STARES

Roy Fuller

25ρ

SINCLAIR-STEVENSON

First published in Great Britain by
Sinclair-Stevenson Limited
7/8 Kendrick Mews
London SW7 3HG, England

044950644

British Library Cataloguing in Publication Data
Fuller, Roy 1912–
    Stares.
    I. Title
    823.914 [F]
    ISBN 1–85619–008–0

Typeset by Colset (Private) Ltd, Singapore
Printed and bound in England by Clays Ltd, St Ives plc.

To
George and Beryl Sims

1

'WHAT's your book?'

Though his marker was well into the volume, Mr Boraston glanced at the spine, whether through forgetfulness, literary inexperience or legal caution, impossible to say. 'Mansfield Park.'

'Ah!'

He laid the book between us on the seat as if, though acknowledging that reading was to give way to conversation, the latter should be confined to art. However, no indication of his feeling about this (or, indeed, anything else) was shown by his pale face and careful voice, in which expression and accent had been scrupulously edited out. Perhaps this was the discipline imposed by fear of suffering clients' interruptions and tales of woe: emotion must rampage behind, otherwise he wouldn't be at Stares. 'The library facilities are feeble.'

'Aren't you enjoying *Mansfield Park*?'

'That isn't the point,' said Mr Boraston. 'There's no range of books between the old ones, mostly classics, probably sold with Stares when the house was in private ownership, and the paperbacks presumably left behind by patients, a very indifferent collection.'

'You can't really expect anything comprehensive.'

'Why not? The fees are very stiff. The emphasis is on self-therapy and the like. The medical equipment, even the staff, is far from elaborate. Why shouldn't there be some non-battered historical or biographical books? One soon exhausts the reading matter brought by oneself.'

'I suppose they'd argue that reading was a solitary activity they didn't encourage.'

'Institutions always rationalize their deficiencies,' said Mr Boraston.

'You don't sound altogether pleased with Stares.'

'I'm certainly not convinced that it lives up to its reputation.'

'Just another case of imagination failing to foretell reality. When I used to hear of someone having had a successful stay at Stares I thought of it as being spelt S-T-A-I-R-S, miraculously raising them from the lower depths.'

No flicker passed over the fine skin of Mr Boraston's face.

'I can see now why my medical insurance people have been so sticky about contributing to the cost of my time here. It would be an exaggeration to suggest an element of quackery or profiteering, but all the same . . . What company are you with, Mr Toyne? Have you had any trouble over your claim?'

'I'm not insured.'

'Well, now you'll have learnt your lesson, if I may say so. Though I suppose the exactions of Stares fall less hardly on an actor than more mundane salary earners.'

'Actors can be as ill-paid as anyone. Besides, it's over six months since I worked.'

'Tch.'

'Luckily I've just come into some money.' I was astonished that this reference to my inheritance slipped so patly out: could it be that Stares' encouragement of confession was already working? I felt my eyes burning a little with the old tears, but pressed further on the sore. 'An unexpected legacy that enables me to pay my way here.'

'Not the most satisfying way of blowing in a windfall. Though when you get to my age life will have told you that our hoardings have to go not on pleasure but mere survival.'

'Obviously you still have faith in Stares, in spite of the library's shortcomings.'

'The library would be low down on my list of complaints,' said Mr Boraston. 'More important to my mind is the absence of Mowle. You'd imagine that in a Resident Medical Director residence would be an essential element.'

'Someone said he was on holiday.'

'That is not so. I particularly asked the Deputy – who was otherwise quite vague.'

'It was actually Dr Stembridge I saw when I arrived.'

'There you are,' said Mr Boraston. 'I don't suppose you've ever clapped eyes on Dr Mowle.'

'No, that may be part of the therapy. You can't expect to communicate with God at first. Did you ever see an old silent film called *The Cabinet of Dr Caligari*? Sometimes turns up on TV.'

'Not to my knowledge.'

'The sinister figure that terrified the community turned out in the end to be the Director of a lunatic asylum.'

'This isn't a lunatic asylum, Mr Toyne.'

'Of course, it's true the sinisterness was simply in the mind of one of the loonies.'

'We shall only be able to judge Dr Mowle's persona when he deigns to appear,' said Mr Boraston.

We were sitting by the small lake that was separated from the terrace of the original red-brick Victorian-Gothic mansion by a slope of garden and lawn bounded by a wall. It struck me that indeed our situation resembled the opening sequence of *Caligari*. All that was required was for a feminine form in white to appear from the rhododendrons. 'They say there's an old man on one of the upper floors who sees ants running over everything, even the food.'

'Not very likely,' said Mr Boraston.

'No, at least the hygiene of Stares is beyond reproach.'

'I mean not likely that a patient in such *extremis* exists here,' he said sharply.

'Some of us must be in worse shape than others. There are bars on a few of the windows up there, as you can see.'

'They were probably nursery rooms in the old days. I remember bars on the window of my own room as a child.'

'They seem rather too plainly symbolical.'

'What do you mean?' Mr Boraston asked. 'They existed merely to protect children from their own follies.'

'There you are.'

'I must say I used sometimes to worry that my own children might fall from a window – among other dangers that occur to over-conscientious parents.'

'At Stares one begins to see most things as symbolical.'

'I'm afraid we outside the artistic world are more literal.'

'All of us here are encouraged to look into the past. Even more than into the future.'

'Yes,' said Mr Boraston, leaning forward a little, bridging his knees with clasped white hands. His suit, though by no means tweedy, could be regarded as a concession to his present state: a weekend or even holiday garb, never seen in his office. As he spoke I once again observed the gold inlays on the lower teeth, the gold wires of bridgework projecting slightly at the side of the upper; rather Frankensteinian evidence of prosperity and care. 'And I've come to think that's right,' he went on. 'Not that one didn't – before – look all too often into the past. But – I believe what one has to do . . .'

'Is to look into the past previously skipped.'

'Yes, I used to think I was a happy man. Now I think of myself as unhappy. The latter concept is just as erroneous as the earlier.'

'Is that Dr Stembridge's notion?'

'Not at all,' said Mr Boraston. 'I've never found Stembridge had two ideas to rub together. Even though one seeks the support of a place like this, one has one's own insights.'

'Even so, one can't help feeling happy or unhappy.'

'The mistake, Mr Toyne, is drawing the general conclusion.'

'I wonder if it isn't simply waking up in the morning and discovering whether or not there is something to look forward to.'

'I almost wish it were as simple as that.'

Suddenly I was struck with an interest in his corporeal presence. 'When did you change from happiness to unhappiness?'

'Recently, when I lost my wife.'

He didn't go on. I was surprised he'd said so much, wearing his waistcoat in the warm sunshine, a pen and gold pencil visible in one of the pockets, quite as though he'd agreed to see a client at home on a Saturday morning, perfectly equipped for normal life.

'I expect bereavement has brought most of us here.'

He nodded assent, and then said: 'Who's that coming towards us through the rose garden? I've left my distance glasses indoors.'

'Mr Charley.'

'I thought so. Shall we move on?'

'With pleasure.'

He picked up *Mansfield Park* and started without apparent haste but with long strides round the lake. I hadn't realized before how tall he was.

'You find Mr Charley boring?' I said.

'Distasteful.'

'He seems to tell everyone precisely how he comes to be at Stares.'

'I wouldn't necessarily find frankness distasteful.'

'He's inclined to gloat over the details.' I said. 'And somehow his name seems apposite, like a character in a seventeenth-century play.'

'A proper Charley?' Mr Boraston questioned.

'The low connotations of Charley are multitudinous.'

'Social intercourse is best conducted without the intrusion of the physical.'

'Except between those in love.'

'I wonder,' said Mr Boraston.

I was taking perhaps four steps to his three. The disadvantage of small stature came home to me, as it has so often in my life. How many actors, actresses too, were near-midgets, ranting and showing off, like bogus Napoleons or precocious children, to compensate for their lack of size! Spending their youth cultivating essentially incongruous big voices and big gestures. Dressing-up often even in private life, in elaborate arrangements of clothes and hair, however inappropriate their physiques, like puny monarchs compelled to wear ceremonial or military garb. It was comforting to think that a big man like Boraston could also be dotty.

'I wonder,' he said again. 'But I'm sure you'd think me utterly superannuated if I pressed the argument. Not to say unbalanced.'

'We expect to find the unbalanced within these walls.'

A surreptitious glance showed Mr Charley far in the distance: a few more strides took us into the greater safety of the trees that lined the path along the stream. There was the metallic sound of leaves falling, even in the calm air great numbers of them, glinting occasionally in the sunlight the boughs admitted.

'It was my second wife I lost,' said Mr Boraston, with no change of tone. 'We weren't at all close. It was only when she'd gone and I remembered former times that I realized how far from close we'd become. A young man like yourself may have no notion how formal an intimate relation can grow. In any case, we men don't normally live in the past, do we? It seems to take some shock to bring the past home to us. I'm senior partner in a busy practice and for a good few years I've taken my share of public duties. I enjoyed my professional life. I was proud of my professional organizations, my town. Why couldn't all that continue after I'd been . . . left? Of course, one saw there was going to be a gap, and domestic inconveniences, but the latter were solved quite satisfactorily. I kept my house on, even my little hide-out in the Lakes. And yet my zest for life had gone. When the shock had receded and the disturbances been smoothed over, my motive power had disappeared. The engine was dead.'

'I understand that.'

'Since you're here I suppose you can. I'd no insight myself. It wasn't "like me", as they say. At first one thought in terms of a "tonic". I went to my GP and suggested that to him, minimizing the truth, as one does when actually in the patient's chair. The same phenomenon can be seen in one's own clients. Anyway, it appears the "tonic" has no place in modern medicine. It was rather like asking a solicitor to engross a will by hand on parchment. Not that my man had anything better to offer. Of course, I didn't convey to him at first how utter my nullity was.'

'Not easy to describe, moreover.'

'Exactly,' said Mr Boraston. 'To wake up without the will to face the day, yet finding it intolerable to lie for just a few moments in bed. To fail to find any motive for following the activities one's previous life set in train. But even saying such things doesn't delineate one's state.'

'No.'

'You may be wishing you'd stayed to risk Mr Charley's confidences,' said Mr Boraston, with slightly surprising wryness.

'I think I've heard most of them.'

'Now you've heard some of mine. In future you can take appropriate action.'

The leaves had invaded the path: Boraston's shoes swished through them, a slow beat with a wire brush on a tympanum.

'It's as though you were possessed by anti-life,' I said.

'Anti-life?'

'The negation of all that had brought you to where you were when the thing hit you.'

'I wonder if one's whole life hasn't been out of character,' said Boraston. 'My being here would be quite inconceivable to those who know me. Yet here I am.'

The shoes were black, of old-fashioned style: perhaps they had never before been for a stroll on a weekday mid-morning.

'The margin between inside here and outside may be narrower than generally imagined.'

'No, no,' he said. 'I cling to the sanity and purpose of

what one's done. The years may have been ordinary but surely not pointless. Whereas self-incarceration here . . .'

'Yet in this last half hour something's been gained, unlikely in the outside world.'

'The Charley syndrome's infectious, Mr Toyne.'

'My first name's William.'

'I know that. It's familiar from television. Though stupidly enough I couldn't have fitted the face to the name.'

'This fairly recent addition is confusing.' I passed a hand over my beard and moustache.

'Is that it? Lawyers are often imprecise about factual detail, knowing it can always be looked up when required. Also, there's no doubt one becomes irritatingly vague in one's sixties. I realize it can't be altogether flattering to you to be simply associated with television. But the theatre in my town has long since become a supermarket.'

'Bill Toyne's what I get.'

'I can match that; rather, go one worse. In my case Wilfred has become Fred.'

I wondered, still with unease, but undoubtedly less agonized embarrassment than of old, whether he wasn't suppressing out of tact his knowledge of the brief notoriety conferred on me by the media, not because of my professional accomplishments but through Sammy. Perhaps I would never lose this excruciating sense of every new acquaintance being silently aware of my intimate past.

The curve of the path had brought us in sight of the house again. Across the lake the late-Victorian red-brick looked in the October sun as mellow as it no doubt could ever look. The large windows of the strictly functional extension reflected the light.

'Do you go in for coffee, Fred?'

'I do what's expected of me. Though I choose the Ovaltine or whatever it is, as the less poisonous.'

'Elevenses no better than the library.'

'Worse.'

'Let's cut across the grass, shall we?'

As we went, some jet planes, a feature of outdoor life at Stares, slithered overhead.

2

THE glass doors of the extension had been folded back, allowing access to a paved terrace where a few white tables and chairs had appeared, tribute to the sudden Indian summer. But few patients had taken advantage of the al-fresco amenity offered: as in an expensive hotel out of season the central-heating radiators remained the focus of social life. Fred Boraston had been detained by Mrs Cochrane at the refreshments table indoors. A sparrow descended on the back of the other chair flanking the table at which I was sitting. I crumbled a bit of biscuit and flicked the crumbs across the table-top towards her. The snack was unhesitatingly accepted. I thought of other, now cured or incurable, loonies inculcating the habit during the long spring and summer.

The sparrow vacated the seat in favour of Noel Mummery.

'I hope you're not going to duck my art class this morning,' he said.

'I'm not sure that playing with substitute faeces is what I need at the moment.'

'I'll issue you with some charcoal and you can rough out a few stage designs.'

'Would that be therapeutic?'

'Do you good to get your fingers dirty. But we don't want you to carry your neuroses into art.'

'Isn't that the idea of art?'

'Certainly not,' said Mummery. 'Do you think my

whole life is simply messing about with shite?'

'I don't know, Noel. You tell me.'

He was laughing extravagantly, as he frequently did, so probably missed hearing this. It occurred to me, as soon as I'd said it, that had he caught it and taken it seriously he might well have been offended, for when I'd visited his house in the village the impasto and hues of the work of his on view made the schoolboy word not inappropriate.

When the noise had died down, I added: 'How do you get someone like Fred Boraston to slosh gouache about?'

'I don't as yet. But it'll come.'

'Couldn't you have picked a more agreeable way of earning your living than teaching the dotty to paint?'

'You're not all dotty.' More laughter. 'Besides, I don't teach painting. I just loosen the bowels, to apply your metaphor. I used to teach: that *was* disagreeable. Now, the less talent my pupils have the better. And few of them are young. And I'm Arts Director not Art Director.'

'But don't you feel you want to go off your rocker yourself, being here all the time?'

'Why should I? I've only got a big mortgage and three children and a diabetic missus and my mother-in-law living with us, perhaps for ever.'

Possibly my question had been subconsciously prompted by the glimpse I'd been afforded into his private life by encountering him in the village and his asking me in for a drink. No member of the family had appeared, but there had been something faintly *outré* in the Edwardian semi-detached house, its bareness accentuated by the white interior, Noel's paintings not being hung on the walls but stacked against them.

'You're lucky to be coping with that amount of ordinary life.'

'I've got hidden sorrows as well,' he said. His small metal-rimmed spectacles rested on his cheeks, though the chubbiness of the latter was not fully revealed because of the harshly-curling beard. What would be presented if the face were clean-shaven: a weakling, simpleton, remains of schoolboy nicknamed Fatty? In the coincidence of two bearded men at the one table it seemed to me, quite unjustifiably, that only Noel provided the absurd or pathological element. It was amusing, even faintly alarming, to contemplate my rehabilitation being in the hands of one whose physical appearance had been further made the worst of by dress. The green sweater that disappeared under the beard reappeared at the wrists of the jacket. Boots suitable for a jungle safari vanished up the shapeless cylinders of the purple pants. He wore a little quasi-military cap presumably less from fear of draughts on the terrace than to hide the premature baldness below. He went on, almost as if divining something of my thoughts: 'What are you going to do if you don't come to me this morning? I feel responsible for you. I am responsible for you.'

'Have you ever read *Mansfield Park*?'

'What's that?'

'A novel by Jane Austen.'

'I've heard of her. Wasn't she a man?'

It was always difficult to know, particularly as the evidence was made ambiguous by guffaws (as now), how far his illiteracy was exaggerated – and whether for comic effect or concealment. Presumably he couldn't have escaped all cultural intimations from the college of art I'd heard him speak of with such scorn. 'In *Mansfield Park* the inhabitants of a country house and their visitors put on a performance of a play, with stirring psychological results.'

'No time to produce drama, lad.'

'I thought I might produce, if you're going to call the business that. It would simply be a reading.'

'Great. Great idea, Bill. Carry on producing. But how would we get copies of this 'ere play?'

'The play in *Mansfield Park* was a translation of a play by an eighteenth-century kraut, not likely to engage your patients here. I thought something in paperback might be found in the town. What about Chekhov? *The Seagull* has a manageable cast, and no extras. Extras would absorb the audience. Would you like to mention it to the powers that be?'

'Copies can be paid for out of petty cash.'

'I mean the idea of a play-reading. Even in *Mansfield Park* it had sensational effects.'

'I hereby authorize it. After all, I am Arts Director, as previously pointed out.'

'In *Mansfield Park* the scheme went forward in the absence of the head of the family, with rather dire consequences on his sudden return.'

'I don't think we shall see Dr Mowle back before the play is read, its therapy absorbed, and the cast returned to their own houses. In any case, what's wrong with reading a play? Just the sort of thing I might have dreamed up myself in my enthusiastic days. I must buzz off to my group.'

'Where is Dr Mowle?'

He had risen, was pulling the green sweater down over his largish corporation.

'What are you going to do until lunch-time?'

'Are you worried I'll do something foolish?' Even the boobyish and genial warder never stopped being a warder.

'It's part of the game that you shouldn't be occupationless, as you know. Besides, your wandering about reflects on the attraction of my group.'

'I'll keep out of sight in my room, sir.' As we parted I

thought, not for the first time, of my car in one of the lock-up garages converted from the stabling, unused since I drove it here. In theory I could get into it and drive away – for an hour, for some adventure, for ever. I was astonished at my lack of life's resources, hard to decide whether physical or spiritual.

3

THE likeness of conditions to those at school or during National Service had already struck me, and not merely in the tinge of illegality permeating any activity not being pursued by the majority. The proportions of the bedroom, the occasional noises from next door, indicated its construction from a unit of more civilized purpose, better days, reminiscent of officers' quarters both at home and abroad. From up here the little lake revealed its shape. A moorhen scuttled into the fringing rhododendrons. On the sloping lawn, plying their feverish exploratory activities, were the birds that had given the house its name. No humans were visible: presumably all not incapacitated by such things as imaginary ants had been rounded up by Noel Mummery. The table and chair in front of the window rather compelled one to sit down in order to look out, so I was confronted with paper and notebook, uneasy reminder of obligation to literary activity. Sammy's playing might have been expected to start in the room below.

I could think back to a time when writing was simply a gratifying bonus to existence. Perhaps it was because I'd started when my acting life was assured that the pursuit had been almost wholly unanxious, like a game, the purpose of winning on the whole subservient to the interest of playing. Besides, since it had started as an adjunct to acting there was immediate success – radio talk, TV sketch – the very modesty of which seemed an encouragement to expand and diversify. So what more natural – yet more flattering – when Sammy and I set up house that one of the little bedrooms over the 'music-room' should have been earmarked as my study? But how quickly (as it now seemed) had my occupancy become tainted! Sitting at this not dissimilar set-up at Stares, I felt my body almost take on the same tremors as at number 87; physical movements of rage and, nearly impossible to believe, fear, so that the mere appearance of sheets of paper on a table stood for frustrated ambition, over-run deadlines, prolonged and paralysed gazing.

Yes, in the end I was afraid of Sammy. But how did all the days we were together at number 87 work up to their almost identical crises? Despite their repetitive pattern, comparative nearness, it was difficult to reconstruct their plots, and now one marvelled at their inevitability. Sometimes I willed myself to be conciliatory. Sometimes weariness or low spirits made me passive. Sometimes I at once fought back, even anticipating – perhaps provoking – by a sharpness of tongue the familiar accusations and abuse. Always the same squalid situation was arrived at in the end, not excluding biffing. One saw now that Sammy's obsessions regimented the days; obsessions of a kind one could observe lingering in several of the denizens of Stares. When the episodes were over it might be wondered how they could possibly have come about: then, retracing the steps of the thing, it could be seen that one had contributed nothing to it, that denial of guilt had been nullified by false reiteration of conduct and views simply not held.

The harpsichord-playing came at a fairly late stage in the repetitive sequence. That he continued to choose that instrument rather than the piano was an irony that quite possibly he was conscious of. The point had arisen when fixing on my study. If I stick to the harpsichord while you're working, he said, I'll disturb you less. Beecham's joke of skeletons copulating on a tin roof, referred to by one of us, seemed aptly lubricious. The days soon seemed remote when the sound was welcome, stimulating, a reassurance about my own work – so tentative with pen and paper at a desk – because of its professionalism. All at once my sitting there had become merely a retreat from the impossible conflicts in the rooms we shared, and his performances uniformly fortissimo, consistently insensitive, though even at their most drunken they retained a skill that compelled admiration, induced regretful despair at the degeneration, a taste even then of my present guilt. For it had to be asked what crucial deficiency of one's own had provoked the change in him.

Against all my artistic desires, all the instinct I had about my progress, at the end I took an ordinary commercial West End part, a big role in a little Aunt Edna comedy that ran and ran. Public as well as private life became a parody. I slipped back into the ridiculous tricks learnt in my first repertory job: the delicate mopping of the brow in moments of crisis, hitching the tie-knot to denote embarrassment, the timing of cigarette-lighting and syphon-squirting to enunciate a punch-line. Astonishing to find that the tricks worked (even drawing the cigarette to the lips down the profile, as I'd heard Gerald du Maurier used to do) like ponderous exhibits in an industrial museum, as though all one had thought and learnt about one's art had been irrelevant. But the sense of fear and disaster was usually postponed until late at night, until I walked up the ramp of the Brewer Street garage to get my car, or still later. And even then there was the possibility that when I returned home Sammy would be already asleep, or spending the night away.

I saw through the window, coming round the lake towards the house, Mrs Cochrane and Mary Gow. From this distance Mrs Cochrane, despite her stick, looked younger than I'd imagined her; thin and quite stylishly dressed. The women's direction surely indicated that I might now look at my watch. But the hands had barely reached twelve, though the second hand was still pulsing away. I saw how the need for a drink arose, far, far more clearly than when, almost in self-defence, I'd gone part of the way down the road with Sammy. But I was playing fair, unlike some patients at Stares, notably (I guessed) Mary Gow, whose silences, usually pale, were sometimes slightly flushed high up the cheek bones. Perhaps she had a bottle locked in her suitcase on her wardrobe top, a hiding-place I'd more than once thought of as the only possible one. Since the suspicious staff might well come round and shake the patient's luggage, I'd envisaged a half bottle at a time, muffled with a dirty shirt; in Mary Gow's case possibly a woollen jumper. The two women passed across the distant trees, whose assortment of browns, surely beyond the resource of even the most inventive painter, seemed to exist in a world alarmingly left behind – as the ordinary world appears to someone in great pain. Who could be troubled to enjoy and feel himself part of such a view, let alone depict it? There was a knock on the door. I welcomed it, as postponing evil thoughts, even injudicious deeds, though it might signal only the temporary intrusion of a chamber-maid, or the embarrassing Mr Charley. No response came to my invitation to enter, repeated several times. I got up and opened the door. Paul Vickerman stood there, occupying the height of the frame as though, like a figure in a stained-glass window, designed for the space, and with such a figure's somewhat awkward attitude. Silently, he put an envelope into my hand. When I asked him to come in he took a couple of strides over the threshold, still without a word. I don't suppose he had any idea of the generosity of my invitation. He had called at my bedroom once before, a visit of extreme inconclusiveness. Somehow, through a number of slight encounters, we had formed a relationship of sorts, but he was certainly the most difficult character I'd come across at Stares.

I said: 'I wish I'd have known you were going to duck the art nonsense, too. We could have had an exciting round of clock-golf.'

'I've been occupied. I couldn't have come.'

I had to tell him to sit in the easy chair, where his tallness seemed to become more manageable – for him as well as for me. He had emphasized his stylized elongation by growing an extended though unsuccessful beard, fairer even than his silky hair. Once again I had the sense of the slight mania of whiskers.

'I missed you at the lake this morning.'

'I was occupied then, as well.'

'I took my stroll with Mr Boraston. He turns out to be called Fred.'

No response from the averted face. It always came as a surprise to find him uninterested in gossip, even in others at all. I found myself still holding the envelope, and asked him what it was.

'It's what Dr Stembridge calls a *curriculum vitae*.'

'Stembridge's *curriculum vitae*?' Was the Deputy Medical Director like Noel Mummery, then – apparently not an awful lot less cracked than the patients?

'Why do you think Dr Stembridge should give me his *curriculum vitae*?'

'Haven't the foggiest. To bolster your confidence in him?'

'But it's my *curriculum vitae*.'

'Oh, yours.' As often with the boy, though the exchanges seemed bound to take a ludicrous turn there was no occasion for mirth; rather, boredom.

'Dr Stembridge asked me to write it.'

'Why are you giving it to me?' If he'd said 'because I like you', or whatever, would I have taken the thing further? All the worlds inhabited from time to time, however restricted or inappropriate, must provide an arena for the libido. Nevertheless, in Paul's case his neurosis seemed, as sometimes does obvious erotic inexperience, to guard rather than increase his desirability. Besides, like the dialogues conducted with him, the further one progressed, almost certainly the more tedious things would become.

'I don't know anyone else who would understand it.'

'But you hardly know me.'

'Understand it artistically.'

Gazing at his solemn face, I found nothing to say. Above his great height of brow the hair was already thinning: if he survived he would go into a bald early middle-age.

'I want you to peruse it,' he added.

'Of course I'll peruse it.' The repetition of the absurd word had no effect on him.

'Before Dr Stembridge, you see. You may say I shouldn't show it to Dr Stembridge. It could increase his confusion about me.'

'Maybe his idea is to decrease your own confusion, as in the case of all of us.'

'Not Dr Stembridge. Dr Mowle might do that, but not Dr Stembridge.'

'That's interesting. Fred Boraston also thinks better of Dr Mowle. But his opinion is only theoretical. I presume yours is based on experience.'

'I've only met Dr Mowle once. When I first arrived. I didn't dare look him in the eye then, so I don't suppose I should recognize him now. Except perhaps through his voice, which was . . .' He hesitated.

'You still aren't a great eye-looker-in.'

'But I talk about such things now, Mr Toyne.'

'What do you think has happened to old Mowle – gone underground?'

'To judge by his voice, Dr Mowle isn't much older than Dr Stembridge. If at all.'

'My metaphor was drawn from Shakespeare,' I said. 'Did you ever see a Hitchcock film called *Spellbound*? There, the head of an asylum was murdered by the second-in-command.'

'Is this an asylum?' He looked at his hands intently, an habitual attitude.

'Of course not. There aren't any asylums these days.'

'When will you peruse it?'

I weighed the envelope in my hand. 'This afternoon, I hope.'

'After that, we shall meet again?'

'Of course,' I said, wondering what possible embarrassment lay ahead. He stood up. 'If you wait till I've washed my hands I'll go down to lunch with you.'

While I was at the basin I heard a crunch and thud behind me of inexplicable origin and startling dimensions. I whirled round and saw Paul collapsed across the table. I thought: he's killed himself – and hesitated to go to him, as one might to an injured animal. Some movement, however, quickly came from the sprawled limbs. I took hold of his shoulders and tried to ease him into the chair by the table. A strange – yet remotely familiar – sensation came of an amenable slender body. After what seemed a substantial time, but in reality was mere seconds, he was sitting more or less upright in the chair.

'Please forgive my weakness,' I made out him saying.

'Shall I ring for someone?'

'No, no.' His head was bowed: what his countenance reflected of physical or mental distress was impossible to see. 'Of course, I *am* weak. That is undoubted.'

'I think perhaps I ought to ring. That's what the staff are for.'

'I'm quite recovered now,' he said, and stood up to prove it, though sitting down again almost immediately. 'Some of them say I'm suffering from *petit mal*.' His voice reflected the torpor into which he had sunk.

'Don't they treat you for it?' I realized that though I'd seen or heard the phrase, I didn't precisely know what the ailment was. The episode reminded me of some unidentifiable scene in a play or novel, Dostoevskyan in its ineffable blend of the alarming and the comic – perhaps actually by Dostoevsky. Later, it occurred to me that Paul might have been deliberately re-enacting the original.

'Treat me? No, they don't. Not here.' He spoke like one just wakened from deep sleep.

4

'DOWN the savage captain struck her,' quoted Mr Charley, as our opponents took their fourth trick. His game-call in four hearts had been over-sanguine: indeed, he lost a further trick in the end play. 'Sorry, partner,' he said to me as I notched up the penalty. Since the stakes were a mere penny a hundred, I took the reverse with phlegm.

Our opponents were Mary Gow and Mrs Cochrane: the venue was Mr Boraston's *bête noir*, the so-called library. Indeed, once it had undoubtedly been a library: as noted by Mr Boraston, among the mainly empty shelves behind glass there were a few with the sparse accumulation of books (not excluding paperbacks) left behind by passing patients, and several serried ranks of pretty unreadable and no doubt unsaleable volumes, such as sets, perhaps incomplete, of Lytton and Charles Lever. Some political books possibly indicated the time limit of the place's use as a private house, works dealing with inter-war crises in the Balkans or Near East, humanity now no nearer ending its religious and frontier squabbles – indeed even farther away. Not for the first time in mid-afternoon I found myself a member of a bridge four. Fred Boraston had initially been adumbrated as the other man: then at the last moment, too late for avoidance, Mr Charley substituted himself. I love the game, but Mary Gow was a poor, and John Charley an erratic player, so that even in the rubbers when I drew Mrs Cochrane the contest lacked interest, the opposition being self-defeating. However, I told myself that the activity was therapeutic; an exercise of calm and patience. Besides, what should I be doing else?

Mr Charley dealt the cards. Mary Gow took an unconscionable time bidding. One always had the impression of a somewhat blotched face and smudged lipstick, but on a more careful look neither state could really be descried. Perhaps in the solitariness of her room she wept a lot. If her conduct at the bridge table was characteristic of her response to life no wonder she was at Stares. A couple of days ago her parents had appeared – the mother rather well turned out, the father of military aspect. I wondered at the wisdom of this: visiting of any kind was discouraged, so Dr Stembridge had told me on my arrival, though the family would be brought in if such a move were considered helpful. And Mrs Cochrane had commented to me that no worse happening than the parents' visit could be imagined: 'they are killing her with kindness,' was her phrase. Perhaps Mary had only taken up bridge at her parents' insistence – to try to keep her amused, or to make up a four with some family friend.

At last, instead of bidding she said: 'I'd like to go for a walk before it gets dark.'

No one responded to this, so I said: 'Let's make this the last hand.'

'But we're a game up,' said Mr Charley. In this, as in other affairs of life, he took on an almost infantile persona, pouting a little under his white moustache.

'The rules of bridge cater for the abandonment of a rubber with one side a game to the good. Besides, there's this hand still to play.'

'Well, I hope we're going to play it,' said Mr Charley.

'If Mary wants to stop, let's stop now,' said Mrs Cochrane. 'Mary, do you want to call it a day?'

'Well, I don't –,' the girl began.

'It's Mary's bid,' said Mr Charley.

As Mrs Cochrane pressed her question I saw this trivial but awkward episode as the sort of thing that well might go on in the Gow home, the more serious the further it was prolonged.

'I expect she's got a rotten hand,' put in Mr Charley, not altogether facetiously.

'Now you musn't bully the child,' said Mrs Cochrane. The angle of her sharp nose, somehow even the rather elongated nostrils, suggested to me, not for the first time, a bird. Perhaps one of those that busied themselves on the lawns outside, the house's eponymous stares. Her grey coiffure always seemed professionally done (and indeed one had seen a framed notice in the entrance hall offering the service of a hairdresser), and she wore spectacles of fashionable style. Her voice was deepish, modulated – a bit disconcerting until, in conversation with her, I had found out that somewhere in the north she taught elocution – or speech therapy, as she had sometimes called it. Why she was at Stares had not been made manifest: in fact, *vis-à-vis* Mary Gow she seemed to be falling into a role that might become akin to that of a parental oppressor. She had changed, this afternoon, from the tweed skirt and cardigan of the morning to a dress whose sleeves conveyed a soft, trailing impression somewhat at odds with the conventional hair and spectacles. As so often, one wondered if one's instant summation had really measured the character's dimensions.

'Pass,' said Mary Gow quite suddenly.

'There you are. She probably holds a complete yarborough.'

'Now don't be so naughty, Mr Charley,' said Mrs Cochrane.

I quickly put in my call, in the hope the game would not degenerate utterly into cross-talk. Mrs Cochrane added: 'I'm sure Mr Toyne would tell us that another rule of bridge forbids commenting on the calling.'

'The rules of fair play should take care of that.'

'Very true,' said Mrs Cochrane. 'Two hearts.'

'Passe-partout,' said Mr Charley, making the absurd pun not for the first time. He probably had the yarborough.

The ladies proceeded to a game call, and made their contract. I said: 'That takes care of the unfinished rubber question.'

'Would you like me to come with you, Mary?' Mrs Cochrane enquired.

Mary Gow was already half out of her seat. 'No . . . thank you . . .'

'Hey,' said Mr Charley, 'don't leave us without settling your debts.'

'It looks as though we owe them a little,' I said, totting up the scores.

'Are you sure?' Again, one couldn't quite tell if his parsimonious concern was assumed or not.

When Mary Gow had departed with her pence, Mrs Cochrane said: 'You know you oughtn't to tease that poor girl, Mr Charley.'

' "Poor", "poor"? We're all poor here.'

'At least most of us have had experience of life. Mary seems scarcely to have set foot outside her family.'

'Let's have a rubber or two of three-handed,' said Mr Charley, gathering up the cards. My heart sank at the prospect of participation in that inferior and chancy game.

'No,' said Mrs Cochrane, getting to her feet. 'I shall take this opportunity of writing a few letters.'

She, too, evidently detested the prospect. She picked up her handbag and spectacle-case, grasped her stick and went away with a slight billowing of draperies.

'It looks as though we're condemned to honeymoon bridge,' said Mr Charley.

'I draw the line at that,' I said. With Mrs Cochrane's departure I felt my social obligations had ceased.

'It's not too bad a game.'

'I loathe it. A worse parody than three-handed.'

'Rummy?'

The old-fashioned term dated him, almost endearingly. 'I think not.'

I put my pen away and picked up my own spectacle-case, but before I could rise he said: 'Naughty. She said don't be naughty. That's what I was apropos my case, you know. It was just naughtiness, as a child might be naughty. They didn't look at it like that. It was all taken with tremendous seriousness. Frightening. It was only the sort of thing a boy might do. Well, I did it once or twice myself as a boy. But being sixty-six years old an entirely different view was taken of it. That hardly seems fair. Did I tell you what happened?'

Mr Charley did not stay for an answer. 'You see the girl was my daily woman's daughter. Her mother was ill so she brought my washing. I was picking plums – Victorias, meagre crop this year. I asked her to sit down and eat one or two. This was on a garden seat, in full view. I'd no idea of anything happening. I put my hand up her skirt. The idea was to squeeze her thigh, which in fact I did. You've no idea what a pretty girl she is. Only fourteen, it turned out. A schoolgirl's short skirts. But then skirts are short generally. She was upset. I admit that. And she went home and complained to Mother. So there I was in the police court.' He shuffled the cards abstractedly and expertly. It had to be admitted that his love of cards was somewhat of a virtue.

'Rotten luck.'

'Rotten luck,' he repeated. 'I'm glad you say that. Sympathy has been conspicuous through its absence. The bloody police charged me with indecent assault.'

I had heard some of this before. Why didn't I cut him short? There was no doubt that a strand of the therapy at Stares was the placing of an abnormal clientèle in what a cant phrase might describe as a 'formal hotel situation'. The harmless gossip of a marine Grand or Majestic was here concerned with crime, drugs, family anguish, erotic loss. Who knows whether I might not myself want in a weak hour to confess?

'Would you believe it, I never asked my solicitor whether in fact I'd committed an indecent assault. He was a chap who'd made my will, that sort of thing. Doubt he knew much about crime. He'd got together with the police, and more or less admitted the offence. The idea was that to save the girl the distress of giving evidence I should plead guilty. Then that would be put to the Bench in mitigation. I mean my guilty plea would be presented as a virtuous act. Which it was by Stanford-Smith, the solicitor fellow. And I suppose in a way the thing worked. In the sense that there was a suspended sentence on condition I underwent treatment. Treatment! Well, you see a pretty child's legs and you want to squeeze them. What treatment is there for that?'

'What indeed?'

'But was I really guilty, Mr Toyne? I mean technically guilty. That question never came up. I didn't reach the girl's drawers. The readers of the local paper

never appreciated that. As far as they knew, I touched
. . . the receipt of custom.'

Distasteful as on the whole John Charley was, it had
to be admitted that his story was not uninteresting. It
almost seemed to me that with a less suggestive name
he might have been quite tolerable. From the years of
my early boyhood in the north came the dim memory
of a chamber-pot being called 'charley'. And of a
hunchback being said to carry a charley on his back
(whether a chamber-pot or a pack, unclear). There was
also, as Fred Boraston had pointed out, the more
recent usage of a 'proper charley' to denote a fool.

'I sometimes think,' he went on, 'that the most
disastrous consequence of the case was to leave me
without a daily woman, and not a cat in hell's chance
of getting one. Who in the village was going to come
and risk the chance of an unwelcome hand up their
skirts?'

'It might be wise to move house.'

'I've been thinking about that during my stay here.
Not much else to do, and somehow there seemed no
time before. What an upheaval it would be! You've no
idea. All my dead wife's muck. She died three years
ago but I never cleared her things out. I was going to
leave them for my son to deal with. Make him work for
his inheritance, such as it is. Besides, he almost never
came to see his mother, though she dearly wanted him
to. So it would be a sort of poetic justice.'

He paused, as though contemplating with some
satisfaction his son's discomfiture. I rose and said: 'I
too must go and get through a few chores before
dinner.'

'Looks as though I'm condemned to playing
patience.'

'There are worse occupations. It aids the thought
processes.'

'That's just what I don't want.' I heard him say, as I made for the heavy mahogany double doors, evidence of England's Edwardian riches, now merely an irrelevance to the half cracked.

5

'I was formerly an undergraduate but working isolately in philosophy of the Bishop Berkeley formula. Though my work followed the university school of idealism I was unable to get in touch with the professors and most of all my own tutor. I have now quitted the university. If my stay at Stares suggested by the parents is successful I shall return to the questions of the primacy of the matter or spirit, but accustomed to studying isolately I shall not propose to enter any sodality.

'I was born the youngest to the parents. By now the brothers and sisters have left home, most married. I am debarred from marriage for various reasons and if I do not go back to a university this will present me with problems of working isolately which will be the only satisfactory method of working.

'All my school life I was a devout pupil. That is not the right word, but the capacity for language left me after I was advised to read philosophy instead of the Romantic movements of literature, in which I in isolation saw the connexions or patterns from Shakespeare through to the American rehabilitation of vocabulary. I was never devout as to Jesus Christ nor am I now, yet the regions now cirkumventing the Holy Land are a point of anguish to me, their violence and terror, worse than in Roman days. Surely there is the episenter of the nuclear earthquake to come?

'I saw my Beatrice when I was sixteen years of age,

and watched her until she disappeared whether through the wish to avoid my love, even death, I do not know. Never even spoke to her, or knew her name. But in any case marriage could not be . . .'

I flipped through the remaining three or four pages. They seemed to be much of a muchness, boring when their dotty novelty had worn off; little chronology; no insight, except a parade of obsessions; nothing to be gleaned, as it seemed to me, except that Paul Vickerman was perhaps further round the bend than I imagined – though arguable whether we all wouldn't seem so if we had to compile a *curriculum vitae*. The evidence of study, even of brain-power, among the ramblings was surprising. I pondered what to do when he returned to tackle me on its literary aspect, as he undoubtedly would. Best, perhaps, was to question him about Bishop Berkeley or the Romantic poets, least likely to cause him to collapse again on my floor. Was he merely an extreme case of a university drop-out, or already far on the road to mental chaos, incapacity for living? Stares was a sort of limbo, temporary shelter for souls who might return to life or fall over into incarceration or oblivion. Quite appropriate to put this to Paul, who saw himself partly in Dantean terms.

But wasn't there a certain lack of disinterestedness in turning over Paul's case in my mind, a possible coming together should he, as it were, regain his emotional freedom – a speculativeness absent had it been Mary Gow who had put a *curriculum vitae* in my hands?

I heard in the distance the gong booming that summoned us at lunch and dinner times. Before I went down I looked closely at my face in the wardrobe mirror. Though as a day wore on one progressively recovered somewhat (subjectively, at any rate) from

the wearing effects of insomnia, pallor and dark eye-
sockets often remained – for the unwelcome scrutiny
of third parties; and at Stares, oddly enough, one
wanted even less to display the badges of malaise, as
though the inmates were in some vital competition of
well-being. I wondered not for the first time whether
Dr Stembridge was right in trying to wean me from my
sleeping pills. 'You are in danger of addiction,' he had
pronounced, 'if not already addicted.' 'But they aren't
barbiturates.' 'Addiction is always harmful.' 'Anything's better than insomnnia.' 'Mr Toyne, you are
comparatively a young man. I want to see you restored
to completely normal life.'

But what for me – for anyone? – was normal life?
Quite apart from the elusiveness of the sleeping state,
wasn't my whole orientation 'abnormal', though to
myself not so? When Sammy and I had first set up
house our choice and arrangement of accomodation
were – to appease the 'normal' world – as by two
youngish heterosexual bachelors sharing living
expenses pre-marriage. And then in the end the
physical separation had become an utter necessity.

The discreet central lighting, the candles on the
individual tables, promised a better repast than in all
likelihood would be forthcoming. Denise, the *maître*
(or, rather, *maîtresse*) *d'hôtel* had absolute power to
assign one to a table. Did she collaborate with the
medical staff to achieve some therapeutic purpose, or
was it a matter of her own experimental whims? Her
warm greeting, neat black suit, some unidentified
papers in her hand, also raised usually unjustified
gastronomic expectations. Wine was not served, nor
available: that would, so it seemed to me, have been
therapeutic in the circumstances, but not a few in the
dining-room were being dried out. Denise showed
me to a table with only one vacancy. Fortunately,

Mr Charley was not of its number: there was Mrs Cochrane and a rather raddled woman called Maida Brown, not awfully old, however; and Noel Mummery, who dined in on the evenings when he had to do with the post-prandial activities. Noel was looking Maida Brown in the eye and laughing loudly; she was po-faced. The Arts Director seemed not in the least disconcerted at the lack of response. He turned to me and said: 'Maida would make a very good Masha.'

'What?' The remark struck me as utterly enigmatic; not for the first time one thought of Noel as an inmate, rather than a member of staff.

'Masha. You suggested *The Seagull*, lad.'

'Oh, Masha. I thought you meant an Edwardian man-about-town.'

Noel's laugh burst out again. 'What do they call that? Casting against type?'

'Of course, I wish I knew what you men were talking about,' said Mrs Cochrane. 'You seem to be rather personal.'

'The idea is to extend the arts programme with a play-reading,' said Noel. 'It is right up your street.'

'Yes,' said Mrs Cochrane gravely. 'That is certainly so.'

'Bill Toyne came up with the notion this morning, and with my usual efficiency I secured several Penguins of Chekhov's plays this afternoon.'

'And you sound as though you've refreshed your memory of *The Seagull*,' I said.

'That is correct, comrade.' Possibly Noel really thought Chekhov had survived into the Soviet era, but his facetiousness was unreliably wild.

'As a matter of fact,' said Mrs Cochrane, 'I used to advise a local drama group that sometimes put on a play-reading.'

'Bill says he will produce our affair, but I'm sure he'll be glad of help.'

'I should be happy to step down in favour of Mrs Cochrane.'

'No, no. I defer to the professional; I always have done.' Her eyes, behind the elaborately held lenses, fixed me intensely. 'I respect and admire the professional.'

'But I hope you'll take part,' I said. 'I think we shall rather rely on you.'

'You mean the bloody inmates are going to do this thing,' Maida enquired in a voice no doubt hoarsened by years of cigarettes.

I said: 'There is quite a sound precedent for it – the murder of Marat, enacted by the Marquis de Sade and his fellow patients at Charenton.'

Noel's laugh resounded. 'By gum, I'd forgotten that. Perhaps we should have done the Marat–Sade play. Then Maida could have played Charlotte Corday.'

Maida glared at him, but whether the reference had been grasped was unclear. What she said was: 'Bloody tomato again.' At that moment the soup had arrived at the table.

'Of course, I daresay they buy great cartons of soup powder, so some repetition must be expected,' said Mrs Cochrane. Not for the first time I noted her habit of prefixing her remarks with 'of course', whether appropriate or not. Who was the first dramatist systematically to depict character through a catch-phrase? Jonson? It was telling and amusing on the stage, less so in real life. I wondered how the Chekhov translation procured by Noel Mummery dealt with Sorin's catch-phrases. Surely it was not impossible to find idiomatic equivalents, but how few versions avoided awkwardness and implausibility. It was the same with Gayev in *The Cherry Orchard*:

some translators seemed ignorant of the game of billiards.

'All their cartons surely can't be tomato,' said Maida.

'What have you got in store for us tonight, Noel? Nothing so repetitious as the soup, I hope.'

'Wait and see. For one thing, I shall announce the play-reading, and ask for volunteers.'

'You may have to say "you, you and you".'

'People get used to doing rum things in this establishment,' Noel said. As he took a spoonful of soup I hoped I managed liquids and my own beard more hygienically and adroitly. I glanced across the room to the third beard of Stares, but in a Rembrandtesque chiaroscuro Paul Vickerman was simply staring at his place-mat, having refused or already finished his soup. In any case his beard began down in the hollow below his lower lip, and his moustache was mainly a matter of mandarin-like side trailings. Was he revolving the ideas of George Berkeley? But despite the extreme tenousness of the *curriculum vitae*, through it I felt I knew him more intimately, though real contact with that muddled mind, to which he presumably assigned priority and sovereignty, seemed doubtful of achievement. I felt Noel's eyes on me, and I returned to the soup. Did he think I was pondering a pass at Paul? Once again the question arose as to the extent of the perspicuity beneath Noel's crude exterior. If one ever had to play a painter, *sforzandos* of speech would be in order, and somehow one's hands would have to be made big and white; however high or low the quality of the artistic work, a rough mastery of existence to be suggested.

'Of course,' Mrs Cochrane said to me, 'I felt a bit guilty this afternoon leaving you alone with Mr Charley. I can't abide three-handed bridge.'

'Who'd want to be left alone with Mr Charley?' said Maida.

I felt I couldn't confess that I'd weakly allowed myself to hear further details of his 'case'. 'It was OK. I got out of playing honeymoon bridge. *And* rummy, as he calls it.'

'A honeymoon with Mr Charley,' said Maida. 'What a prospect!'

'He was married once,' I said.

'We were all married once,' she said, looking me insolently in the eye.

'I think I shall go vegetarian tonight,' said Noel, 'and plump for the cheese and mushroom in baked spud.'

'The vegetarian option is often wise,' I said.

Was Noel deliberately saving me from an embarrassing turn to the conversation? If so, his tact was surprising. But possibly the staff were instructed to smooth over any tears appearing in the social fabric. Suddenly, not for the first time, life as ordinarily lived seemed futile, hardly to be undergone, quite without prospect of interest, let alone happiness. Curiously, I was reminded of certain episodes at school, when I had been in hot water or bullied or felt the end of term impossibly far off, in which the feeling-tone had been unalleviated despair. Even then the character must have been formed that could scarcely withstand disaster.

6

BETWEEN the dining-room and the extended terrace was a broad, windowed corridor. A glass double door gave on to the terrace, at this time of day and year kept closed. After dinner, a few went through the door, tempted by the St Luke's Summer. I myself went farther – down the stone staircase to the lawn – having had enough *pro tem* of my fellow patients. Immediately, one was in the half alien, half appealing natural world. Perhaps the play-reading could be given *al fresco*. There was the dim reflection of the lake between the shrubs at the foot of the staircase, apt for *The Seagull*. But it was not likely the erection of a platform could be arranged.

The grass at first was shadowed by the lights from the house; but as I went into the dark I was conscious of being followed. When I turned I recognized the elongated silhouette as Paul Vickerman's.

'Did you read the *curriculum vitae*?'

'I want to read it again. When have you to hand it in?'

'I'm seeing Dr Stembridge at three-thirty.'

'Tomorrow.'

'Yes.'

'Let's have a word after lunch.'

'Do you think he ought to have gone on with his study of the Romantics?'

'Who?' For a moment I envisaged Stembridge reading Keats and Shelley.

'Myself. My old self. You see, it appears to others all too much when the concept of Romantic embraced the whole of English literature. But then what is philosophy if not all embracing? Just as impossible.'

'Philosophy or not, I feel it's a great pity you gave up the university. Where were you?'

'Exeter. I could go to Southampton. Southampton would take him.'

'Why don't you aim for that?'

'I have to be cured first. That's the word used. I expect you think that an impossible condition precedent.'

'Not at all. We're all here to be cured.'

'But how are they to be cured who aren't here? The regions of the Holy Land are full of madmen. You see them on television in processions, and with guns, all dishevelled and shouting.'

It suddenly struck me that the reason television receivers were not supplied to the bedrooms at Stares was not parsimony, as I'd previously thought, but to guard the patients from disturbing pictures – in this epoch, non-fictional in the main. There was a 'television room', well patronized, but I saw now that the choice of channels was supervised, piped from the centre.

'One certainly must be alarmed about that. It's as though the dissentious tribes of the Bible had possessed automatic weapons instead of spears and bows and arrows. Although I expect the peace-lovers of those days were sufficiently alarmed.'

'Don't you think we may be here, in Stares, because we are peaceful?'

I considered the proposition. Was Maida Brown peaceful? 'I don't suppose any of us would fire guns off or form part of a mob. That may be because we are all cowards.'

'The walkie-talkies they use. It's possible to pick up the messages.'

Did he mean here or in Palestine? The sound of laughter came from the terrace, the distance and the open-air lending it a musical effect, like the laughter or conversation one sometimes got on a jazz disc recorded in a club.

'I think we ought to go indoors and see what Noel Mummery has in store for us,' I said. He did not move as I drew up to him, so I took his arm and gently urged him round. The feel of a fellow human still seemed strange after a good many months.

7

A BOVE the steaming surface of the water rose a number of heads, mostly male, mostly motionless. The whiskers of Noel Mummery and Paul Vickerman (to say nothing of my own about to join them) helped to give the general effect of the Emperors' heads outside the Sheldonian, decaying, slightly sinister. Possibly Noel, following his art transparencies quiz tournament of the previous evening (as his Asquithian promise at dinner had proved to be), had slept at Stares. I hung my dressing-gown on a hook and walked down the steps into the water. It was scarcely possible to dive in, as much because of the meagre dimensions of the pool as of the numbers using it. The water, like so much at Stares, was said to be therapeutic; certainly it was curiously warm, though the heat was presumably a good deal boosted. The pool was in the cellarage, constructed by the arthritic shipowner who had built the house. I essayed a few swimming strokes then found myself up against an elderly man whose large bald head contributed to the Roman effect. I had seen him about during the last couple of days.

'Good-morning,' he said. 'My name's Chiswell.'

'I'm Bill Toyne.'

'I know. I've seen you on the goggle-box. I expect everyone tells you that. Not altogether an unmixed blessing, I suppose.' We were at the deep end of the pool, where it was necessary to tread water.

Mr Chiswell's words were punctuated by his rather laboured breathing.

'Many people think one is someone else. A fellow who runs a chat-show or reads the news.'

'I've always enjoyed the theatre. I was brought up in the days of touring companies. Now in my old age I watch drama on the box. In any case, the theatres within reach are run by left-wing loonies, worse than amateurs.'

'Were you there when Noel Mummery talked about the play-reading?'

'Yes I was.'

'Did it interest you?'

'To take part?'

'Yes.'

'Hadn't thought about it.'

'Will you?'

'What?'

'Think about it.'

'Yes.' He allowed the lower half of his face to disappear beneath the water, as though to cover some embarrassment.

'Good,' I said. 'I'll be in touch. Now I think I'll try to swim a few lengths, bodies permitting.'

When I eventually approached the steps at the shallow end I was momentarily impeded from leaving the pool by the press of non-swimmers or the indolent. Just ahead I found Mr Charley. He had lowered his body so that his head was numbered among the decapitated, and with his hands he was making horizontal passes as if treading water, though even one of his short stature must have his feet on the bottom. He was singing quietly, for some reason in a falsetto voice:

From my fond lips the eager answers fall,
Thinking I hear thee, thinking I hear thee call.

I had the notion of turning tail, to set out on another couple of lengths, but in the second of indecision he had swivelled his head towards me with one of his characteristic alert, button-holing movements.

'All right for our bridge four this afternoon?' he asked.

A prospect of enslaved afternoons opened up.

'Unfortunately I've arranged to see someone after lunch. Don't know how long it will take.'

'We might squeeze a rubber or two in in the morning.'

'I shall be tied up with that play-reading affair.'

'I might have to go at that myself,' he said.

'Report as instructed.' I saw an opening and launched myself for the steps. As I waited for the lift, Mr Chiswell joined me, also dressing-gowned. We exchanged remarks about the lift's characteristic tardiness.

'Do you think it's a part of the original fabric, like the pool?'

He gave this serious consideration. Now revealed in its entirety, his figure was inclined to stoutness, no more than my own height. The mild set of his features and long upper lip gave him the look of a prelate, an effect enhanced by his white towel filling the neck of his dressing-gown, like some accoutrement of High Church costume. The dressing-gown itself was of thick monkish material, cord decorating the lapels and sleeves – the sort of garment sold by school outfitters.

We were the only two in the lift. 'First floor?' he enquired.

'Yes. Most of us seem to be there. Though they say there's a bad case in one of the attics.'

'I wonder how they judge a bad case here. We all seem to talk and eat and sleep in a reasonable way.'

'I don't know about sleep,' I said.

The lift ascended apparently in a series of jerks, the mechanism effecting this difficult to envisage. Quite suddenly he said: 'I was in the Istanbul Airport shooting.'

'Good Lord.'

'I'm supposed to disclose this when appropriate. For therapeutic purposes.'

Again, that word. 'There's no doubt one's natural curiosity is heightened in this place.' He would be curious about me, though (like many) may have read the newspapers about Sammy's inquest. But how could I follow with my troubles that appalling act of terrorism in Turkey?

'Apparently I wasn't recovering from it – mentally, I mean. So the quack suggested I came here.'

The lift gave a final clank. Its lattice had to be yanked back in order to emerge through the landing's door. 'I've been here rather longer than you,' I said. 'If it's any comfort, my judgement's not altogether adverse, though it still strikes me as a pretty rum place.'

We paused for a moment in the corridor. 'Sometimes,' he said, 'it seems just a mediocre hotel, such as one used to come across more in the past.'

'The guests, too, rather fall into that category.'

'Yes,' he said. 'Present company excepted.'

'No. No exceptions.'

He laughed. It seemed rather virtuous that I should have drawn some amusement from him.

8

BREAKFAST was a matter of self-service. On tables joined in the centre of the room were ranged various cereal packets, like a small but monster-volumed juvenile library. There were jugs of fruit juices, presumably canned. In the covered recesses of a hot-plate was a choice (or amalgamation) of scrambled eggs, bacon, and sausages, more palatable than might have been expected. As so often with English institutions, breakfast was the repast Stares did best. There was no Denise to ensure that the patients 'Observe degree, priority and place, Insisture, course, proportion, season, form, Office and custom, in all line of order.' I noticed Paul and Mrs Cochrane together at a table, he talking to her with surprising freedom. I had picked up my bespoke newspaper from the desk in reception, so made for an empty table.

On the front page of *The Times* was a large photograph of a crowd of robed and head-dressed Semites, clenched right hands shaken high (like a professional footballer after scoring a goal), a coffin bobbing about among them. No asylum was comprehensive enough in modern times. It could be argued, looking round this quiet room, that it was the saner who had incarcerated themselves.

On her way out Mrs Cochrane stopped by. 'May I sit down for a moment?' I rose and pulled out a chair. 'I saw you in the garden last night with Paul,' she went on. 'Possibly you're quite close to him.'

'Well, I thought you were, too. Over the breakfast table just now.'

'He told me you were in the swimming-bath this morning.'

'That's right.'

'Of course, he often speaks very strangely. I felt I ought to tell someone what he said before it went out of my mind. He compared the swimming-bath with the Underworld.'

'Have you been down there? Rather an apt comparison.'

'I haven't ventured there myself. Swimming has never appealed to me.'

'It's more soaking than swimming.'

'Paul said that underground water was the place where the Devil might lurk, in the shape of Leviathan, the Adversary. The embodiment of the force of Evil.'

I actually speculated as to what wickedness might fill those imperial heads: perhaps only the illicit desires of their near-nude but hidden bodies. 'Did you take it that this was fanciful or that he really believed it?'

'He gives you the impression of being absolutely serious all the time, poor boy. These were the times of the triumphs of the Adversary, he said.'

'Well, who can deny that?'

'Yes,' said Mrs Cochrane, 'but is it sensible – sane – to put it in Paul's terms? I worry about that boy.'

Her tone, her physiognomy, her tense attitude, invested the conventional phrase with unusual feeling. I think for the first time I saw her as one with the right to be at Stares – her expensive spectacles, changes of conventional dress, catch-phrase, slightly absurd occupation, an initially effective but eventually penetrable disguise for an altogether more vulnerable and feminine persona. And, after all, she wasn't old: in any case, however our own experience may contradict it, we're apt to write off too soon the desire and ability of both men and women to form the ardent attachments of youth. I was turning over whether or not to tell her about the *curriculum vitae* when she continued: 'I wonder whether he's getting the right treatment; whether it's . . . rigorous enough.'

'Dr Stembridge isn't a fool, and he's very experienced.'

'I'd be much happier if Dr Mowle were available. I don't think a great deal of this young man who's appeared lately. What's he called? Pentecost.'

'I'm due to see Stembridge this morning. Shall I mention Paul to him ?'

'I do wish you would. The doctor doesn't always see the most of the game. Paul may keep his Leviathan and suchlike to himself in Dr Stembridge's presence.'

'I suppose we all keep something to ourselves.'

'Yes,' said Mrs Cochrane, 'but for the vast majority of us the regime here is perfectly adequate – relief from domestic worries, from our relations, a change of scene, surroundings really tranquil and quite lovely, medical advice and concern on tap, as it were. It's been very much borne in on me since I came here how ugly my normal ambience is. Well, perhaps not uniformly ugly, but indifferent – indifferent to human need.'

'I can't remember where you live.'

'Crewe,' she said. The mock tragedy of the monosyllable promised well for her participation in the play-reading.

'That's where actors' paths used to cross on Sundays in touring days.'

'I wish I'd been among them,' said Mrs Cochrane. 'But all I managed to do was to try to change Crewian accents. My parents would never have let me attempt the stage. When I was absurdly young I married an estate agent who turned out to be very successful, and then lost him, with too much of my life unexpired.'

'I was brought up in Liverpool and thereabouts. And I had an accent to change.'

'But you escaped, Mr Toyne.'

'Please call me Bill.'

'My name's Lorna. That dates me a bit I'm afraid. I suppose my parents remembered Blackmore's novel.'

'Was that when the name came in?'

She fiddled with a rather nice ring. 'I shouldn't have said "escaped". I was happy with my husband. In fact, looking back, amazingly, fortunately happy. We can't appreciate happiness at the time, when we're young.' She looked up at me. 'You must remember that. You're very young to be here.'

I felt myself reddening. 'I had a . . . grisly experience.' The curious word popped out unawares. Was that what I thought of it all?

'But you'll get over it. It will merge into the past, I can assure you.' She rose. 'Now I'll leave you in peace with your coffee and newspaper.'

'We must talk again,' I said.

'I hope we shall.' Her cardigan was merely thrown over her shoulders: its sleeves whirled away as she left me, plying her stick, a touch of the thwarted thespian.

9

THOUGH quite a few turned up for the 'casting session' for the reading, most were those I'd already got to know, including, surprisingly, Fred Boraston, who said he was not unused to spouting in public, having done quite a bit of advocacy in his more youthful days. Noel Mummery was there, taking charge, plainly regarding the operation as part of his 'programme', perhaps to perpetuate it with future generations of patients. When I'd looked at the play in bed the previous night I found I knew it quite well. I'd played Yakov (or Jacob, as it had been transliterated in the programme), almost a mere walk-on part, at the Arts Theatre in my earliest West End days. Yakov, one of the workmen who erect the stage for the performance of Constantin's 'play within the play', has a few lines, not really characterized, but I'd milked them by giving them a Liverpool accent.

We had gathered in the so-called White Drawing-room. Already there was a subdued excitement, so familiar at the outset of a theatrical enterprise; not unakin to an occasion when children 'show off'. After some chatter and self-deprecation we'd cast the thing, though still needing a Dorn, a Yakov and a Polena, the estate manager's wife. I told them how the reading was to be done – no action, the readers sitting in a semi-circle, the sharing and over-looking of copies of the play to be worked out. The aim was a couple of read-throughs, if possible, then the public reading on

Sunday. It had not struck me till then that even before and between the read-throughs a certain collaboration among the cast was required by reason of the shortage of copies. No doubt this would be thought 'therapeutic' under Stares law. As I remarked to Noel, when the others had left, play-readings might become standard practice in such institutions, providing temporary jobs as producers for 'resting' actors.

'Well,' he said, 'it remains to be seen whether it does good or causes bust-ups. I've known rows about relative skills break out among those first starting to paint. Great calls on the painting-therapist's attention.'

'Oh Lord.'

'Watch out for that Masha.'

As Noel had prognosticated, Maida Brown had been cast as the estate's manager's daughter, hopelessly in love with Constantin, who is hopelessly in love with Nina, who is disastrously infatuated with Trigorin, who is loved by Madame Arkadin . . . It occurred to me at once how immediately pre-Stares Chekhov's world was. The logical end for most of the characters might have been to remove them from the anguish and complications of their lives by sending them away for a 'cure'.

'I hope the fuse to some explosive device isn't being lit there,' I said. I'd forgotten the doctor's saying that Masha was 'off to down a couple of glasses before lunch'. Then later in the play she says to Trigorin, 'Women drink more often than you think.'

'Well,' said Noel with a laugh, 'there's nothing very startling these days about that remark. Women booze nearly as much as men now they've got jobs and money.'

'Maida may not care to utter it in public.'

'I don't think Maida much cares what she says.'

'There may well be other time-bombs in the text. I

shall bowdlerize it thoroughly. Luckily I told them I should have to cut it because of the time involved, so there will be nothing invidious in leaving bits out.'

'I was surprised Mary Gow agreed to take part,' said Noel.

'I think Mrs Cochrane brought her in. It seems she was quite a star in her school plays.' Mary was going to read Nina: one wondered about her stamina.

'She's a very pretty girl,' Noel said.

'Do you think so?' The proposition was slightly surprising.

'Nice and busty.'

Did he know of my tastes, and was he teasingly testing me out? Yet again his behaviour presented a choice of subtlety or naivety. As we moved from the room he said: 'Do you feel like an illegal drink? There's plenty of time to get to the pub and back before lunch.'

'Sorry. I'm due to see Stembridge at twelve.'

'Another time.'

I left him and ascended the absurdly mahogany-rich staircase. On the landing, opposite Dr Stembridge's door, was a row of chairs and a low table on which magazines were laid out. The dark wallpaper had been lightened by a series of modern prints, mainly abstract, perhaps sold by the dozen. Nevertheless, the feeling as one sat down was of waiting outside the headmaster's study for some reprimand, even painful punishment. On the door-frame had been affixed a device which by shining a green or red light indicated whether one was to enter or not. I was early: the red light shone. I sat down and turned over the pages of *Good Housekeeping*, stopping at an article on Yorkshire regional cooking. The brief recipes given were just what would have interested Sammy in his cooking days. 'Sheffield Fish Scallop' was simply cod fillet sandwiched between raw potato cut to the same size, dipped in a batter and deep fried. As I took this in, Mrs Stogden emerged.

'You didn't come to the play-reading meeting,' I said in mock accusation as I rose.

'Well, I knew I should have to leave in the middle of it because of my appointment. That would have seemed discourteous, wouldn't have been understood.' She took my remark seriously – a nervous woman, on the borders of middle-age, intelligent. She had seen me several times in former days at the Old Vic; we'd conversed about the company and the plays. She had a good memory for the actor's art.

'Will you take part anyway?'

'If you want me. I shouldn't be any good.'

'That's not the point.'

'All right.' Her black hair was worn piled up on her head. Some wisps had descended, perhaps denoting an arduous session with Stembridge.

'The part of Polena is going.'

'Is Polena the woman –' she hesitated.

'The estate manager's wife, in love with the doctor.'

'Oh yes,' she said. 'Didn't I once see a real-life Pauline play the part – Pauline Jameson?'

'Could well have been.'

'I may just be making that up. Association of ideas. The result of a session with Dr Stembridge.'

'Really it wasn't until I glanced at the play yesterday and started casting it that I realized that all the characters were frustratedly in love. Amazingly impudent of Chekhov to work that idea so exhaustively, though somehow there's no impression of repetition when the play is given.'

'I suppose if you looked into all the characters in this place you'd find more or less the same thing.'

I pondered that. 'The difference is,' I said, 'that this isn't a closed world. It would be very awkward if we were all unrequitedly in love with one another.'

'Awkward enough if some of us were requitedly in love with one another,' she said.

For the first time I thought of the possibility of Stares romances, rather like shipboard or holiday romances, needing no more than a few days to blossom, even ripen. Had Mrs Stogden anyone – even herself – in mind? Despite the encouragement given by Stares to revelations by the patients, I'd never learnt her history.

'I expect there's a good response to the play because of the propaganda that goes on here about getting back to normal life.'

'That may be so.'

'Otherwise, who would want to make a fool of herself in public?'

'Nobody will be made a fool of,' I said resolutely.

'Which part will you take?'

'It looks as though I shall have to hog the play by taking the novelist, the Trigorin, though if a volunteer turns up I shall play Yakov.'

'I don't remember Yakov.'

'He's one of the labourers who puts the stage up for Constantin's decadent play.'

'Oh, you must have a bigger part than that.'

'The big actor cheese often chooses a little part, all the better to display his ego. Didn't Garrick play Abel Drugger? Sir Frank Benson in the end used to play the Ghost in *Hamlet*. Hello, the light's turned green. I must enter in my own character.'

'What shall I do about the Polena part?'

I told her about the availability of copies of the play, and the time of the first meeting of the players, and opened Dr Stembridge's door.

It was a classic summoning. He was at his desk, writing – presumably the notes on Mrs Stogden's visit – and nodded me into the chair opposite. By his blotter, facing me, was a sort of toy – a small oblong bath of oil which could be stood on its sides so that variously-hued fluids were drawn down by gravity in various and variously colour-reinforced globules. Evidently the device had just been turned upside down, for there was a quite spectacular (if diminishingly so) display going on of shapes and colours. Was he trying to hypnotize or merely divert his patients? At length he almost threw down his pen, a rather obese fountain-pen.

'Well, Mr Toyne, I hear you're going to treat us to a dramatic spectacle.'

The slight facetiousness was in headmasterly character. It was not easy to resist falling into the role of pupil. 'We may be about to undermine your therapy by involving your patients in Slav melancholy.'

'Our methods can stand up to any amount of play-acting. In a sense, we want our guests to play-act.'

Not for the first time I was struck by his solution of the problem of referring neutrally to the Stares' patients. 'I hope you'll come and hear them.'

'Of course, of course.'

'We're rather frightened, like many theatrical companies, that the *dramatis personae* will outnumber the audience.'

'With you in the cast I'm sure there's no danger of that, Mr Toyne.' He took up the fat pen. 'Now, what have we to add to our story?'

Even in Noel Mummery's attitude traces could be seen of the inability in hospitals and the like to treat the inmates as adults, perhaps most marked in nurses, who generally regard the younger in their care as imbeciles, the older as senile. Though his clients, unlike those on the National Health, had to be relieved of cash, Dr Stembridge's attitude held something of the same.

'I'm sleeping badly. I miss my pills.'

'Let me see,' he said, opening the blue file he'd taken from the top of the several at his side, 'you're on –'

'One Benquil every other night, if requested. And I do request it.'

'Actually, I had in mind to increase the weaning process.'

'I very much hope you won't do that at the moment.' It crossed my mind that I could leave Stares at once, and go back to my friendly GP, who seemed to have no notion of the dangers of addiction.

'Any adverse symptoms?'

'Just insomnia,' I said, but the irony did not strike home, the profession not expecting irony from its clients.

'No intolerance to bright lights? Dizziness or headaches?'

'No.'

'You see, if there are no withdrawal symptoms we are right to persevere with the reduced dosage. Will you try it for few days longer?'

'All right.'

'You can come and see me any time, you know. No need to wait for your regular appointments. Just have a word with Sister.' He directed his charm on me, possibly quite ingenuously, though one was a paying customer, and it could be hazarded that he had a financial interest in Stares beyond his professional remuneration. I guessed he would appeal to women more than men. His dark, chalk-striped, double-breasted jacket failed to camouflage a bruiser's shoulders: at medical school he had likely been a rugby forward. The hair was well-cut, brushed back with a judicious amount of dressing, the features regular – a long-time breaker of nurses' hearts. Apropos Dr Mowle's absence, the not uncomic notion struck me that, as in *Measure for Measure*, the ruler had merely feigned to leave, in order to test out his perhaps suspiciously handsome and virtuous second-in-command.

'You know,' Dr Stembridge said, 'your initiative – which Noel Mummery had told me about – your initiative in the play-reading is an indication of the progress you have made here.'

'Do you think so?' Quite suddenly a warmth flooded my breast, and a less detached view of Stembridge formed itself.

'I've no doubt at all. You probably can't recall your state of mind when you arrived. Such forgetting is commonplace. But I can assure you that your enthusiasm for any theatrical enterprise was nil. You were disillusioned about your talent. These things quite apart from the lingering trauma of the personal tragedy undergone.'

'I still feel I shall never write anything, perhaps never be sure enough of my lines ever to take a part again.'

'But you are going to appear in this play.'

'I shall have the text in my hand.'

'But when you leave us here there will be many such opportunities to ease you back into professional life – verse reading, radio work.'

'You make it sound easy.'

'I don't mean to,' he said warmly. 'No one knows better than someone in my position that the psychological – what can be called the artificial – barriers to success are more formidable than any other.' The toy by his left hand was quiescent. He turned it upside down so that the coloured streaks and rondures began slowly to descend again. 'What about the dreams?'

'Fat lot of chance I have for dreams.'

He laughed. 'I believe it may well be that despite insomnia you are dreaming – and I mean remembering your dreams – more than you've done for months.'

Strangely (for it had not occurred to me), he was right. Just before final wakening, in the hour or two of sleep bequeathed after far more hours of sleeplessness, I had been dreaming with a fantastic inventiveness probably not equalled since adolescence. And Stembridge's words revived vague fragments of a dream of this very morning, and one in which Sammy had appeared – but merely in a minor role and in the slim persona of the time of my first knowing him. Since we spend so much of our lives asleep, why don't we remember more of our dreams?

My mind had wandered off. When it returned to the matter in hand, I heard Stembridge saying: 'About your Benquils, we don't impose a tyranny here – that is a precept of Dr Mowle's – but I'm relying on you eventually to dream without them.'

Once more I saw the *Measure for Measure* parallel. The Duke had let things get too slack, knew it, brought in Angelo, the 'man of stricture and firm abstinence', to enforce the harsh law, and then absented himself. And once more my feeling for Stembridge reverted to its former ambiguity. Angelo was personable and outwardly virtuous by definition –'There is a kind of character in thy life That to th' observer doth this history Fully unfold.' His fallible nature remained to betray itself.

Eventually, to conclude the session, Stembridge – his usual practice – offered me his hand to shake, though another session was booked for the day after tomorrow, to say nothing of the chance of my encountering him in Stares and its purlieu. As I left him, I fell to thinking of the Duke himself, the absent Medical Director. Was he somewhere on the premises, beholding his deputy's sway? I ought to have told Fred Boraston, concerned about the matter, to be on the *qui vive* for an eavesdropping friar.

10

I suppose I let Paul down. I had read completely through, in preparation for his coming (as arranged) to my room, the *curriculum vitae*. My genuine feelings about it were debarred expression through the conventions of politeness and the sense that, after all, it was the business of Stares, not mine, to plumb and ameliorate his derangement. Even some minor aspects seemed impossible to broach: were the occasional strange eccentricities of spelling a function of his illness? They seemed odd in one that a couple of universities were prepared to take, though I recognized that in present times immaculate spelling was no more looked for from the young than immaculate clothes or grooming. One was conscious, too, of unease at the possibility of his once more suddenly fainting – if that was how his previous collapse could be defined – rather like the enforced company of an untrustworthy animal. Still, on this occasion he seemed less *outré* – not only than the prose of the *curriculum vitae* but also as evidenced by the conversations I'd had with him before. His account of being a well-behaved son, head boy at school, innocent of causing any trouble or anxiety in the past, was reasonably coherent. For one thing, there were fewer of those disconcerting third-person references to himself.

I could only counsel him to work towards getting himself fit to go back to university life. Why not accept the presence of fellow students, and the academic view of the subject of his studies, which surely should be English literature? 'On the whole,' I said, 'I'm quite impressed with Stembridge.' The silent questioning, behind the pronouncement, of absolute authority, seemed to me a sufficient sharing of the boy's rebelliousness (if it could be tamely called that). 'That he wants to know about you on your own terms is surely a sign of his sympathy. I'm sure it's right for you to trust the Stares regime.' My own sense of progress, felt during my session with Stembridge of the morning, was a confirmation.

It was hard to tell whether anything one said had any effect. He sat in the easy chair, illuminated by the window's light, features solemn, eyes downcast, the twin channels of premature baldness already indicated. Would he survive to grow bald? That was by no means sure. Even his voice had a finicky wispiness that contradicted the confident vowels of his accent, the latter a legacy from his father, who turned out to be a retired Royal Navy Commander. I asked him if he'd managed to see one of the copies of Chekhov's plays that were going the round of the cast. He had not, and he didn't know *The Seagull*. 'Your role, the Constantin,' I said, 'has written a play that in Act I the characters start to act – a play within a play, like *Hamlet*. Then Constantin's mother, who's a famous actress, pokes fun at it as being decadent. But we hear enough of Constantin's play to indicate that it might have been labelled Modernist rather than decadent. Isn't this rather your territory, the late developments of the Romantic movement?'

But it was tough going. 'Early W B Yeats and Wallace Stevens,' he said, at length, 'the changes are there. In *their* plays also.' It was as though he were reproducing something he had been taught – not so much because of the content of his remarks (which afterwards I realized were utterly apropos) as the unemphatic manner in which they were uttered.

'I've never read Wallace Stevens's plays. But there's surely a good essay to be made out of what you've just said. You *must* start up again at university.' There was a sense that most of one's words hit an absorbent barrier before reaching his ears. 'It's funny that Chekhov put a Modernist play within a play that has proved so popular. He might have done the reverse.'

Paul rose. 'I have to see Dr Stembridge now. Could I have my manuscript?'

I picked up the *curriculum vitae* from the table, and handed it to him, standing up myself, still nowhere near approaching his stature. 'Thank you,' he said. 'And thank you very much for reading it.' It was the automatic response of the well brought-up son, *très comme il faut*. I thought: the hell with it. Why should I have to take on the woes of others when I had enough of my own?

When he'd gone, the strangeness of the play within a play in *The Seagull* was reinforced by my recalling reading somewhere that the arrival of Modernism had announced the separation of culture and society. How cleverly Chekhov in his mature work had avoided Modernism without succumbing to the *vieux chapeau*! Surely that was what every artistic generation had to try to do. It could even be said that at first Chekhov's plays were in truth in danger of being minority art, but then their rational form and ordinary human content won through to audiences almost as wide as those for the dramas of Pinero or Somerset Maugham. I should have raised all this with Paul, to encourage his apparently fading intellectual side, and, above all, to augment the tenuous connections between us – for his fingers, as it were, were slipping through mine like a Hitchcockian ledge-hanging sequence. Though whether any measurable response from him would have ensued was doubtful.

Outside, the St Luke's Summer held. I took the Chekhov volume and went down – out beyond the garden, on to a fairly useless but pretty bridge that spanned a short arm of the lake. I stopped to look into the water, where a mallard swam from under the arch. Looking down on it, I saw that the legs moved adeptly in the fluid, the foot shaped like, and almost as resilient as, a leaf, a view rarely achieved. On the far side of the bridge was a bench, sheltered by rhododendron bushes, on which sat Mr Chiswell, examining something in his hand which, when I came closer, I saw was a dead leaf. When we had greeted each other, with his acquiescence I sat down beside him. When I asked him if he'd decided about taking part in the play-reading, he said yes, he would. I told him the part of Dr Dorn was still vacant, and passed over my copy of the plays. With one hand he still held on to the leaf.

'The seasons go so quickly. Strange how the skeleton sometimes emerges,' he said, letting the leaf fall at last. 'Probably through the wind blowing the leaf about till the softer parts gradually wear away.'

'Rather like the human body.' As soon as I'd uttered this observation I regretted it, for outdoors, in the light of the declining sun, he was plainly even older than I'd imagined.

'Yes,' he said, 'we wear out. Gradually, for the most part. But there are sudden droppings-off and so forth, like the leaves. The same thing seems to apply to the brain, though you're not old enough to have experienced that.'

'Oh, I don't know. The mere fact of being here proves that something untoward has happened upstairs.'

'No, no – you're young till you're seventy, if you're reasonably lucky. Then the business begins to bite. That's what I found.' He flicked the pages of the book with his thumb. 'I can't remember Dr Dorn.'

'You're a bit old for him. He's fifty-five.'

'More than a bit.'

'He's a womanizer. Always singing snatches of songs.'

'You should have cast Mr Charley in that role.'

I laughed. 'So you've heard him warbling Tosti and the like.'

'Being here's rather like being in a play,' he said. 'You get to know people just well enough to be highly conscious of their idiosyncrasies.'

I went on: 'Dr Dorn is loved by the estate manager's wife. She wants him to run away with her, but he isn't having any.'

'Who is going to play the unrequited wife?' he enquired.

'Mrs Stogden.'

'Mm. Personable.'

I laughed. 'I think in real life she too has a husband, perhaps doesn't want to leave him.'

'Oh,' said Mr Chiswell, 'I'm far too old for any kind of amorous adventure, though I'm free – alas, alas.'

'Were you married?'

'My wife died seven years ago.' The leaf had only drifted as far as the space of bench between us: he picked it up again and studied its anatomy. 'I was a headmaster. Lived for years in the school house. When I retired we moved to a country cottage we had, as we'd always planned to do. And there we lived as though time was of no account, as though for us it was standing still. We did – what's the phrase in *As You Like It*?'

'Fleet the time as carelessly as they did in the golden world.'

'That's right. But suddenly up comes a brutal blow and one realizes time has never for a moment stopped madly revolving. The diagnosis of my wife's illness – final illness – was such a blow.'

His lower lip and voice became unsteady, and I saw tears brim his eyes. I looked away, but was moved myself rather than embarrassed.

'Old men cry easily, as someone said.'

'I expect we all cry easily in here,' I replied.

'Are we all melancholiacs, depressives? It seems too simple a diagnosis.'

'It's the Chekhovian view of existence. I was only thinking earlier today that all the characters in *The Seagull* are hopelessly in love, destined to land eventually in a place like Stares.'

A cat emerged from the nearby bushes and trotted towards the house. Mr Chiswell, whose countenance had recovered its ecclesiastic calm, noticed it and said: 'It seems from studies made that town cats kill more birds and country cats more mice, as you'd expect. I wonder which category that moggy falls into. Stares must almost be town for cats.'

'I read somewhere that cats kill a hundred million birds and small mammals every year.'

'What a slaughter! It doesn't bear thinking about. Yet I keep a cat myself.'

'How will it fare while you're away?'

'Physically, all right. There's a cat-flap and a neighbour comes in every day to put food out. Emotionally, I guess badly.'

'Ah, that difficult side of life.'

'I'm not too happy myself about being absent. But at least I know I'm going to return.' Mr Chiswell turned on me his still moist though startlingly blue eyes.

'I'm afraid I've been inflicting you with my concerns exclusively. What about you? This must be a very unwelcome interruption of your engagements – career, even.'

'Yes.' I looked away. 'If we meet again under similar circumstances I may inflict my concerns on you.'

'I wish you would. Dialogues seem to be part of the Stares therapy. Though whether deliberately so, who knows? In any case, few encounters are as congenial as ours has been.'

In the distance several figures, mostly by now familiar, were moving across the lawns towards the house. 'It must be tea-time,' I said. 'Shall we go in?'

'I suppose so,' he said. 'Do you think that stale madeira cake will turn up again?'

'Extremely likely.'

11

'I'D no idea there was a table.'

'The amenity was mentioned in the brochure,' said Fred Boraston, who after tea had asked me if I played snooker.

'I must have missed the reference.'

'Solicitors are trained not to miss things in documents.'

The billiards table was situated in a one-storey annexe, evidently designed for it at the time, or soon after, the house was built. The roof was of glass, rising to a modest peak. The table lights were suspended from horizontal iron members. When they were switched on, a cat was disclosed asleep on the green cloth, the same cat earlier observed moving purposefully over the grounds.

'Not a good augury for the table's condition,' said Mr Boraston. The creature hung limp as a mass of dough when he picked it up, then was reluctant to stand on its feet.

'Have you had to leave a cat problem behind?' I remembered my conversation with the other elderly widower.

'Worse. A dog problem. My daily woman wouldn't take her on so she's had to go in kennels. For the first time, and I worry about her constantly. It makes being here more than ever an indulgence.'

'I'd hardly call it that.'

'Selfish is perhaps the word. Why can't one get back

to normal simply in the company of one's dog?' He had taken a couple of cues from the rack and was rolling them on the table. They undulated. 'I doubt we shall find a reasonably straight implement here.'

'Do you play much?'

'Quite a bit these days. I go a lot to the club.'

'I expect we shall find you will have to give me a few blacks to make a game of it. I'm only a casual player.' I thought of the days when I first joined the Savile, rejoicing in its facilities, feeling membership was part of professional success, playing with Sammy, then giving him lunch, setting up house with him still a tentative prospect of further happiness. The attitudes round (and even half climbing on) the snooker table, compelled by the varying positions of the snooker balls, are curiously pornographic, all the more so for the player being fully clothed and innocent of provocativeness. 'I used to think I was becoming not too bad, but I never kept it up.'

'Shall we just toss a coin to decide who breaks?'

We did so. After his shot he said: 'Who'd believe the cloth could be so worn yet the table so slow. It's like playing uphill. Gilbertian.'

I said: 'This is a moment when one could do with a drink.'

'Yes. The most enjoyable games of snooker in my life I played in India during the war. I was given honorary membership of a local club. Automatically you had a marker-wallah, and just pressed the bell for a fellow to come and take your drinks order. I drank bottled beer in those far-off times, such was the strength of my bladder and digestion.'

'I suppose there's nothing stopping you having a hip-flask, unless you're here to dry out.'

'Nothing at all,' said Mr Boraston. 'And whisky's now my tipple, as they say.' He stooped to make his shot. He had removed his coat revealing, an appropriate waistcoat, buckled at the back; the immaculate cuffs of his shirt were fastened with plain gold links. When I'd taken off my own coat I'd been compelled, waistcoatless, to tuck my tie between two buttons of my shirt. It was like discovering at dress rehearsal that one's costume was sadly inferior to a fellow actor's of similar standing.

'I say, you're going to make mincemeat of me.'

'Bit of a fluke, that.' He took the easy colour he'd left himself. 'I love the single malts. Ideal for a flask, since they're best taken neat. I've never possessed a flask, often thought of buying one, but it seemed too indulgent.' He potted another red. 'Funny about self-indulgence. Though I prefer the single malts and can well afford them, I usually find myself at home with a bottle of proprietary blended.' The blue then went in. 'Have you ever tried Highland Park? It's the most northerly whisky.'

'Quite romantic!' I wondered how long the break was going to last. I was relieved to see him miss a red along the cushion to one of the top corner pockets.

'Yes, distilled in the Orkneys, near Kirkwall. Peaty, rarefied. I used to see the bottle in the club, which prides itself on its range of scotches, and sometimes treated myself. But it was years before I ordered it from my wine merchants. Oh, bad luck!' He re-chalked his cue and dispatched the red I'd left. 'Strange, even exciting, to handle the bottle from my own drinks tray. Perhaps you know it. Rather squat, old-fashioned, the sort of bottle smugglers used to smuggle. Black and gold label round the neck testifying to its age.'

'You're making me more than ever feel the need for a drink.'

He laughed, and missed the black, again going for a

top corner pocket. 'These pockets must have swollen jaws.'

I failed again, and as he stooped for his next shot he said in a rather strangulated voice: 'What do you know about Maida Brown?'

'Absolutely nothing.' Had Fred Boraston conceived an amorous interest in the woman? I was staggered slightly. She would be a tough nut for Boraston to take on. 'She's not one to call a spade a gardening implement.'

'No, I can see that.' As from the balls on the table, the overhead lights were reflected from his tonsure when he got down to play. He stood up and moved his score along with the tip of his cue. While his eyes were turned away, he said: 'You may think this is absurdly fanciful. I had a daughter called Maida. Unusual name today, even at the time.'

' "Had" a daughter?' I was flummoxed by this turn to the conversation.

'I mean she's probably still alive.'

'I see,' I said, but merely to encourage him.

'My first marriage was dissolved. Though my wife was the guilty party – as things went in the law in those days – she had the custody of the only child, a daughter, Maida. The fellow she was in love with worked for Nestlé. He was transferred to the company's place in Vevey, in Switzerland. My ex-wife and Maida went with him.'

While he spoke, I'd time to take a red and miss a colour. There was a silence as he played a shot. Then he went on: 'The war came. I was in the territorials. Eventually went to India. Absolutely lost touch with Vevey, never a strong contact at best. After the war I sometimes thought I'd go out to Switzerland, or perhaps just make enquiries of Nestlé. But I married again, and the old life stopped having any meaning, even the possession of a child. Now my second wife is dead all the past returns. This Maida is about the age my daughter would be. She even resembles my first wife a little.'

I thought: Mr Boraston who had seemed so level-headed, is as bonkers as the rest of us. I said: 'That's Shakespearean, not Chekhovian.'

'It's not quite as far-fetched as you might be thinking. It could have been the child was never told of my existence, was given her step-father's name, all connections lost in a foreign land in wartime.'

'Why don't you ask her about her childhood?'

'She's daunting.'

'Yes,' I said. 'But she would probably come clean and clear the thing up in a few minutes.'

'I suppose I don't really want to clear it up.'

'A dream child. "We are not of Alice, nor of thee, nor are we children at all . . . We are nothing, less than nothing, and dreams." '

He rested the butt of his cue on the floor, and looked at me sharply. 'Yes. Yes. Who wrote that?'

'Charles Lamb. I did selections from *Elia* for an examination at school, and learnt whole passages off by heart. I was a good study in those days. Not so now.'

Mr Boraston's reveries had not affected his prowess at the game. He ran up a break of twenty-two. I said: 'I should need at least three blacks to give you much of a contest.'

'We'll see when this frame is over. I hope you'll find time to do this again. I've enjoyed our talk, as well as the game.'

'Me, too. I feel we've come a good way since we talked about *Mansfield Park* – when was it?'

'Only yesterday,' he said.

'Time seems to gallop yet stay still at Stares. Now all

of a sudden we've got a *Mansfield Park* set-up of our own.'

'You mean the play-reading?'

'Yes.'

'Shall we have to face any morally dubious situations,' he asked, 'as when they proposed to play *Lovers' Vows*?'

'Not in the laxer moral climate of today,' I replied with equal mock seriousness. 'I say, it's only just come to me that if we were going to do *The Cherry Orchard* instead of *The Seagull* you could have played Gayev, the character who's always using billiards phrases –"in off the red" and so forth. If we'd been acting it you could have given authenticity to the movements.'

He dispatched another red. 'My goodness, I nearly went inappropriately in off the red then.'

'That seems the only way I shall score any points.'

12

THERE were lavatories in the basement at Stares, on the same level as the strange swimming-bath. The men's establishment, at least, was generously proportioned, with chequered floor-tiles that revealed bravely their hundred-odd years' life, seats to the WCs almost as generously timbered as the main staircase, and an occasional touch of the original plumbing – some lead pipes, affixed to the wall with *fin-de-siècle*-decorated lead strappings. I was joined at the three-man stall by Mr Charley, humming to himself. Soon he broke into words.

> And I'll find a little cosy corner
> In the heart of the girl I love.

The last word had a final cadence. He said: 'We used to have the sheet music for that song at home. It bracketed "girl" and "boy" as alternative readings, so that the song could be sung by a member of either sex. D'you see?'

'Yes, I see.'

He chuckled. 'Nowadays the issue might not be so clear-cut. I mean a boy might well sing "in the heart of the boy I love".'

I made no answer to this; wondered if he had started that particular song deliberately. I moved over to the washbasins, where he soon joined me.

'This fellow I take in the play, what's he like?'

'His wife loves someone else.'

'Does that tell you much about him?'

'What d'you think?'

'Who's his wife?' Mr Charley asked.

'Mrs Stogden.'

'Hard luck on him.'

'Yes, indeed.' Thus I demonstrated my appreciation of feminine attractions. 'He's the sort of estate manager who only grudgingly supplies amenities for the estate owner, if at all.'

'When I was a boy we used to have a cook who was terribly parsimonious with the food. She wasn't making anything on the side; just accustomed to being canny. Came from Dundee.'

At the roller-towel apparatus, a modern feature, I said: 'He also arranges for the seagull to be stuffed.'

'So that's how the seagull comes in. Sounds a rum play.'

'I think you'll find it quite comprehensible and down to earth.'

We made our way together to the White Drawing-room, where Noel Mummery had arranged the seating so that a sufficiency faced a small table by the fireplace at which there were two chairs where he and I were to be seated. As I took my place, people were still coming in from the end of dinner, some carrying cups of coffee. He had rescued a copy of the Chekhov from one of the players, and put it on the table.

I started by trying to reassure them about the acting skills required. Clear, measured, audible reading of their parts was all that was demanded. 'As a matter of fact,' I said, 'after a couple of runs-through I expect the play to become pretty well characterized simply because of the appearances and voices of those reading. People perhaps don't realize how much a script, to take on life, relies on human beings inhabiting it. In that, it's quite unlike a novel.

—73—

'As you'll have seen, the first two Acts have a setting resembling the gardens here – in the second Act, the lake is actually supposed to be visible. The last two Acts take place in the house.'

At this point, Maida Brown's hoarse voice came from an inconspicuous place she had taken deep in a chintz-covered armchair. It augured well for her reading that it effortlessly established itself. 'Some of us haven't had the chance to investigate the setting or anything else about the play.'

'I'm hoping to get a few more copies tomorrow,' said Noel, at my side.

'Can't you stop the copies we have being monopolized?'

'I'll try to ensure there's some passing on of copies after this little meeting.'

'Not before it's time.'

As in the professional theatre, it was the bit players, not the stars, who caused the trouble. I explained that I was going to make a good few cuts, which could be carried into the other copies on the first read-through. Would people start objecting to their parts being truncated, I wondered? Quaintly enough, in this odd ambience the familiar atmosphere of hundreds of rehearsals began to be perceptible. This would certainly intensify the following morning, when, as I told them, the usual 'art' hours would, in their case, be devoted to the start of the readings.

'Is my gouache of the lake to remain unfinished?' Mr Charley facetiously enquired, not liking to be out of the picture for long.

'Many great masterworks of art have stayed unfinished,' said Noel, laughing his laugh.

Apropos Maida Brown, I speculated as to Fred Boraston's view of her intervention. Of course, he was of an age to experience not only the possible great difference in mature character between his child and himself, but also that such a child's destiny could be sadly disappointing. Who would want to claim a Maida as his own? Well, probably everyone at Stares would like to wind themselves back to a pre-disaster time, even knowing of the suffering to come.

The White Drawing-room meeting did not last long. As I moved into the square central hall – impressive in the dim artificial lighting, despite its mock-baronial style – I found myself detached from Noel, and walking by Mrs Stogden, whom the subdued light also glamourized.

'Have you had a chance to look through your part yet?' I asked her.

'Yes. I may be one of those reviled by Mrs Brown.'

'No doubt the whole project will provide a vehicle for grievances to be aired, steam to be let off. Probably good for us. You'll have to develop a performer's elephant skin.'

'Steam is what I'm short of,' she said.

'I know the sensation.' We had halted by the large table in the middle of the hall – Victorian-Jacobean, like its ambience – on which reposed the visitors' book, brochures, bowls of flowers and a few periodicals of the kind outside Dr Stembridge's office. 'Shall we carry on into the garden and get some air? Will you be warm enough?'

'I've got a shawl with me.'

I opened the massy lock of the great front door: the timber moved surprisingly easily on its hinges. As in Act II of *The Seagull*, the lake glistened, but under the stars, not the sun. We moved down the curving stone stairs.

'I always hope to see the Orionids,' she remarked, 'but never do.'

'What are they?'

'The October meteors. Too early in the night at the moment now, and rather too early in the month.'

'I've never in my life heard of them.'

'They're dust from Halley's Comet.'

'Is that how you pronounce the name?'

'Yes,' she said. 'Even astronomers get it wrong.'

'You sound to be something of an astronomer yourself.'

'I got it almost all from a marvellous mistress at school.'

'What a lot from that sort of source stays with us during life!'

'This sounds like a dialogue from *The Seagull*,' she said, laughing.

'It's like the world seeming Dickensian when you read Dickens.'

'Not quite,' she replied.

'No, not quite. Chekhov's nearer to life. Well, nearer to ordinary life.'

'You mean,' she said, 'our lives – we at Stares – are more exaggerated than those in Chekhov?'

'I suppose so, if we came out with everything.'

'But on the whole we don't,' she said.

Some of the lights from the house became obscured by bushes, but, as one's eyes grew used to the dark, walking down the path posed no problem. I thought that Mr Charley at least came out with everything. 'I hope I haven't let you in for some awkwardness,' I said, with slight guilt. 'You know Mr Charley's playing your husband.' I wondered if she knew of his criminal past. One doubted if he was as free with his legal reminiscences with women, as with men, but I felt I ought to give her the chance to withdraw.

'He disclosed that at the meeting this evening,' she said.

'He was quick off the mark. I only told him just before we went in.'

'Oh, I can cope with Mr Charley.'

'He's an admirer of yours.'

She laughed again. 'Did he come out with that, then?'

'He firmly implied it.'

There was a brief silence before she said: 'I'm used to attracting unsuitable men.'

I let another silence elapse. She broke it by saying: 'When I married I acquired a rotten man as well as a rotten name.'

'If I may say so, Stogden doesn't suit you a bit.'

'Thanks.' Again she laughed. 'I always hated my first name but at least my maiden name was OK.'

'What was that?'

'Hathaway.'

'Shakespearean,' I said, for the second time of the day.

'Yes, but I never really thought of it in that connection. It just seemed to me . . . melodious, dignified. Then Stogden. But of course at first, in love, I didn't think much – if at all – of the name I was going to take on.'

'What's in a name? As the very chap said.'

'More than you think,' she replied.

We had come almost to the lake, where the path turned and curved along its edge. To the right, invisible in the darkness, was a movement and what one fancied to be a slight splash, perhaps a water-rat, or some water-fowl still abroad. Far in the distance, headlights of cars on the road sent up occasional illumination, like the marsh lights of the stage direction in *The Seagull*.

'I stuck with my marriage far longer than I sensibly should. The reason was a cliché – for my daughter's sake. *He* stuck it because I had some money. Well, stuck it with the alleviation of affairs on the side. At last we broke up. The irony was, my daughter was already done in. The cliché had been invalid. I say, this is a terrible imposition on you, Mr Toyne.'

'Not in the least. On the contrary, I appreciate your confidence.' The somewhat Jamesian turn to my words brought home the part I seemed to be playing at Stares – the detached observer, outrageous emotions diluted by his judicious mind and balanced prose style.

'The dark is a great encourager of confidence.'

'I was in the garden last night with Paul Vickerman. I wish he'd confided more. Nothing seems to come from him except strangeness.'

'But we're all strange here,' she said. 'That's why we've come.'

'You don't strike me as strange.'

'Nor do you,' she said, laughing once more. I thought that her readiness to laugh disguised a profound sadness, but possibly that was another cliché.

'Some maintain a veneer of ordinariness,' I said. 'An example of the sort of thing that isn't revealed is the ghastly effect of nights of insomnia. Or perhaps a little pallor is half noticed, not thought of any significance.'

'I wouldn't care to be the mother of Paul Vickerman.'

'He's madder than most.'

Suddenly she burst out: 'Would you believe it, I saw my daughter by accident in Piccadilly Circus, standing on the Eros statue steps. She had her hand resting on the shoulder of a man not young, drinking from a can, in a black leather jacket, with outrageous dyed hair. She was sixteen. I was in the sort of bus you can't get out of except when the driver releases the exit doors at a stop. But then what would have been the use of confronting her? I mean I guessed from her absences – supposedly at my ex-husband's – her style of dress, her appearance, the sort of company she might keep. But that was the start of the end as far as my observation and knowledge went.'

'How truly harrowing!' I dared not ask the child's fate.

'The end of me, too,' said Mrs Stogden.

'No, no. The fact that you can come out with all this betokens a future.'

'Do you really think so?'

'I begin to think so. I begin to think Stares works, in some unlikely way. Otherwise, why does it continue to get customers? When I first talked to Fred Boraston he was full of complaints about the library and the defection of Dr Mowle. Even in a couple of days his concerns are deeper, more – therapeutic, to use a Stares word.'

She evidently pondered this. Eventually I said: 'Ought we to walk back? Despite your shawl you must be cold.'

We turned, and soon the house lights became visible again.

'What *is* your first name?'

'Heather,' she said, laughing.

'Not too bad.'

'Do I look like a Heather?'

'You mean it's a broguey, tweedy name?'

'Or redolent of English perfume.'

'Is there such a thing?'

'Lavender water, wild flowers from the Lakes.'

We strolled on. 'Dust from a comet,' I said. 'What poetry!'

13

IT was not the only dialogue involving feminine confidences I had that night. Much later, in the Red Drawing-room, the more used of the two, I found myself drinking a non-alcoholic night-cap within conversational distance of Lorna Cochrane and an old bent lady, also with a stick, a Miss Stittle, pretty scatty, verging on the gaga. This person was quite soon helped off to bed by the night sister.

'Poor Miss Stittle,' said Mrs Cochrane. 'She loves a chat, but I wonder how long establishments like this will take her. The geriatric ward or home is her fate. I don't myself want to live into that epoch, do you?'

'I haven't thought about it much. Despite everything, on balance I like being alive.'

'Ah, but you're young.'

'Not that young. Don't be deceived by the hair.'

She said out of the blue: 'I see you as someone of great sympathy who has never quite had that sympathy returned.'

'Deep down, I do believe my mother had sympathy. She just couldn't express it.'

'I'm afraid we most easily express disagreeable emotions,' said Mrs Cochrane.

What I'd said about my mother had tripped from the tongue, but I wondered if I'd ever actually thought it so concisely and concretely. Undoubtedly, if my mother had lived on I would have treated her differently, given her opportunities for expression and expressed myself.

Or would I? Could the nature of our relationship have so changed?

'Your mother's passed on?'

'Some years ago,' I said.

'And your father?'

'He's still alive, but we rarely meet. He used to work abroad for most of the year. We were never close.'

'Of course, you were virtually orphaned. It is a sad state, and those who suffer it by no means always realize the extent of their misfortune. The ills that assail them in later life they put down to more recent events. Were you an only child?'

I admitted it. The *tête-à-tête* was less like having one's fortune told than being auditioned by some 'psychological' director. What she had said brought to mind the years of my northern youth, most of them almost prehistoric. We must have lived near Liverpool – latterly Southport – because of my father putting in there, his time of sea travel. I saw the great sands of Southport, myself wandering over them alone. Probably Mrs Cochrane's implications were correct – one was laying up trouble, though presumably battling through the years unremarkably.

'Shall we have another drink?'

Mrs Cochrane had to repeat the question, my mind had wandered so far.

'Yes, all right. Let's be devils.' I got up and pressed the bell by one of fireplaces. At this time of night, as in an hotel, service was provided by the night porter, an elderly individual known as Walter. 'What's your tipple?' I asked, echoing Mr Boraston.

'Ovaltine,' said Mrs Cochrane. Needless to say, alcohol was not available.

'I'm not at all sure those milky beverages suit me.' A year or two ago, I thought, I would never have made such a middle-aged remark.

'What do you have?'

'I discovered you can get Bovril. Not a bad fluid.'

'Of course, I haven't had it since my schooldays. Or was it Oxo we used to have at supper-time?'

'When I was at school I thought of what at the time seemed a brilliant advertising idea for Oxo. A slogan: "Oxo, the original square meal".'

Mrs Cochrane laughed. 'Very good.'

'I found out Oxo's address, and actually wrote to them accordingly.'

'Did they give you any money?'

'They never even acknowledged my letter, as far as I remember. I see now that "square" is wide of the mark, but "cubic" wouldn't have done at all.'

'What strange things one does in childhood!'

'And later on in life, as well,' I said, 'unless one has time to ponder. Even then . . .'

Walter appeared, and I gave him the order, having it put on my account.

'It was my idea,' said Mrs Cochrane. 'I should have paid.'

'I'm surprised they bother with such trival items. You wouldn't think them worth the accounting trouble.'

'They all go through the machine, like the charges for pills.'

'It's strange to think of the business side of this place, only revealed by hints or accidents. Somewhere there must be an office, with non-medical staff beavering away.'

'Of course, Dr Mowle,' said Mrs Cochrane, 'has probably got caught up in the administrative side, and that is why we never see him.'

'Have you ever seen him? Fred Boraston hasn't, and he was here just before me.'

'No. But I'm happy with Dr Stembridge.'

'What lady wouldn't be?'

She laughed. 'Oh, he isn't my type in that sense.'

Walter returned with the drinks. 'I'll just take your old cups away. And move your spectacle-case a wee bit, madam. Your newspaper I'll put on the ledge under the table – don't forget it.' I'd noticed before his habit of giving a running commentary on his actions, at first irritating, now not without interest in seeing how far in absurdity he would go. 'That gives a little more room next to the book for the Ovaltine – I think that was madam's order. I'll put the Bovril here, so you can reach it, sir. And I'll remove the empty biscuit plate which I'm sure you're done with.' He made some concession to the formality of his job by wearing a rather crumpled light-blue jacket, with pearl – or pearl-like plastic – buttons.

'Did you mention Paul Vickerman to Dr Stembridge?' Mrs Cochrane enquired when Walter had gone.

'I'm afraid not. When it came to the crunch I felt I'd no standing in the matter.' The fact was Paul had gone completely from my mind during my session with Stembridge. 'As it turned out, I saw Paul again after we'd spoken about him. In some ways he made me feel more optimistic. Behind that eccentricity there's certainly a mind of sorts, possibly even a good one. But all kinds of unsuitable accretions have grown up round it.'

'They are probably his defence system against his parents. And even against his tutors or professors or whatever they were.'

'He seems to be quite interested in taking part in the play-reading. Well, acquiescent anyway, which perhaps is as much as can be expected. He may come through it with a more conventional, an easier, give-and-take with his fellow humans. At the moment he's living in a world by no means altogether real.'

'I wish I'd had a son to bring up,' Mrs Cochrane said. 'I know I could have done it successfully. From my husband I got a settled life, happy on the whole, and enough money left to me for comfort when he passed on. But no child. I wouldn't have let Paul get to the state he has. It's all a question of upbringing.'

'I wonder if that's so in every case. There's sometimes a bad seed – chemical imbalance, an ancestral gene of dottiness reasserting itself. What can be done about those things?'

'Love and firmness and attention from the earliest childhood on,' said Mrs Cochrane firmly. 'That's the secret.'

She may well have been implying that she could have brought me up, too, and kept me away from Stares. I was wondering why so sensible a person herself was in such a place, when she said: 'My sister is coming to visit me tomorrow.'

I wondered at the breaking of the unwritten no-visitors rule. 'Does she live near here?'

'No, she lives with me in Crewe.'

'Noble of her to come all that way.'

'If you see us together, break in on us.' Her lower lip trembled so much with sudden feeling that her articulation, usually so precise, was quite unsteady. She vouchsafed no explanation but gathered her stick, spectacle-case and, remembering Walter's instruction, her newspaper, said good-night, and went off.

At once, though I wouldn't have said her company meant much, the long-familiar sense of depression fell on me. Future life held nothing of importance or pleasure. And I knew I should not sleep. I drained the Bovril, amazed I should have troubled to order it.

14

BUT I did sleep, and though waking in the night, in the end dozed off again. In the morning I found on my bedside pad a note of the dream I'd had before my mid-night wakening. It ran: 'Strange dream of my troubled headmaster – where is the womb? – just below the navel isn't it? – I take pity on him and have him in my bed.' The intervening sleep had made the note all the more enigmatic.

Yet it seemed to me, as I read the note, that the world I'd wakened to was almost as strange as the one I'd quitted. When I drew the curtains I saw the sun, still low, behind distant trees already nearly bare, sprigs-of-parsley shaped. The lake was gloomy, milieu for Henry James's Quint.

The headmaster I'd dreamed about was a feared figure, remote from all associations with self-doubt, let alone the carnal. He it was who in the dream had raised the question of the womb's location. The second question was my reply. Having him in bed was for his comfort and anxiety, quite unerotic. But the abundant further details of the dream were just beyond recall. Meagre material for Stembridge, though he would triumph about sleeping sans pills. The wandering womb, I thought, was an apt subject for dreaming in a place where hysteria abounded.

After breakfast, waiting for the time fixed for the read-through, I saw Paul Vickerman sitting alone where Mrs Cochrane had sat the previous night. I thought I ought to rally a member of my cast probably prone to unconfidence, and went to sit by him.

'I see you managed to bag a copy of the Chekhov,' I said, flicking the book that lay closed on his knee. It was odd how one slipped into fourth-form expressions talking to him. 'I shall expect great things from you at the rehearsal.'

'Aren't you confusing yourself with William Toyne?' he said.

I stared into his eyes. 'But I am Bill Toyne.'

'So you are,' he said, after a moment or two. 'What a funny thing – I thought you were somebody else.'

'There are several beards about,' I said, facetiously trying to smooth over his disconcerting mistake.

'Well,' he said petulantly, 'I was hoping to see you. It's really the play I'm confused about.'

'What's the trouble?'

'You asked me to read the part of Constantin, but the speeches seem to be ascribed to Trepliev.'

'All Russian names are confusing. When you read, you must think of yourself as Trepliev. When the other characters speak you are Constantin or Constantin Gavrilovich.'

'I have to be a split personality,' he said.

His words and face were deadpan, but I wondered if he wasn't aware of their inner meaning, like my dream of the uncertainly-placed womb.

'Your ears should have burned last night,' I said. 'Mrs Cochrane was talking to me about you at this very table. She takes a great interest in you.'

'I like Mrs Cochrane,' he said. Though his tone was unconvincing, it was possibly the first human commonplace I'd ever heard him deliver.

'That is reciprocated,' I said.

'I like Mrs Cochrane far better than my own mother.'

The tone had grown in intensity. I said lightly: 'That

may or may not help you to read your part as her son in the play.'

'Having to peruse the play has confirmed that my mind is ruined.'

Through the Red Drawing-room's open double-doors the inhabitants of Stares could be seen going about their post-breakfast activities, some no doubt already making for the location of the read-through. All of them could have come out there and then with a remark like Paul's, but nevertheless it had a chilling incongruity. 'So's mine for that matter,' I replied.

'Where's his promise, his achievement? So they might say.'

'My dear boy, you simply haven't had time to spoil your promise.' I stood. 'Come along, curtain up.' He rose obediently, but without the trace of a smile on his long countenance. Had he ever had a sense of humour, even a slight geniality?

In the White Drawing-room Noel had had the requisite number of small uniform chairs arranged as the actual performance would require. They had obviously come from some store, perhaps relics of musical evenings of Stares' private past. I pulled one chair out and sat in it, facing the semi-circle. There were no defaulters, maybe a tribute to Noel's organizing power as well as an indication of the limits of Stares' attractions. By lunch-time, having got them through the first Act, I realized things would have to be speeded up if we were to give the reading on the day planned. For one thing I had to stop tinkering with the text – not the cuts, which were soon indicated, but amendments to the translation. It was not too bad a version, but translatorese lingered, especially in key phrases and catch-phrases, or so it seemed. The opening lines of the play, where Masha enters with the schoolmaster who loves her in vain, went:

MEDVIEDENKO: Why do you always dress in black?

MASHA: I'm in mourning to match my life. I am unhappy.

What the Russian was I had no idea, but I couldn't resist making the exchange nearer to natural English, to make sure – so one thought – of getting the audience's immediate attention:

MEDVIEDENKO: Why do you always wear black?

MASHA: I'm in mourning for my dead life. I'm just not happy.

Sorin, the owner of the estate where the play is set, has two catch-phrases which in Act I are barely established, at least by the rather unresourceful translation. I changed them to 'and all that sort of thing', and 'and that sums it up'. I wasn't sure the latter version was much improvement on the text we had, but it was more striking.

The conjunction of the fictional characters in their real-life personae was what could be termed piquant. Noel Mummery, as the penurious schoolmaster whose love is unreciprocated, was, in a way, cast against his personality. Noel couldn't be imagined as loving in vain; rather, as a bold sexual initiator. Yet what came out strongly was what one suspected ruled his painting: clumsiness and non-success. He spoke his lines quite well. His *vis-à-vis*, Maida as Masha, had the voice if not quite the looks for her part. Though she was not actually wearing black, her habitually sombre clothes fitted that opening line quite well, and she conveyed a bored bossiness very much in character. When it came to Masha's snuff-taking, I thought she might well in real life have sniffed something stronger.

Boraston, as Sorin, was surprisingly effective: little

attempt at dramatizing the words, but a clear, dry delivery. Lorna Cochrane as his sister, the Madame Arkadin, gave almost too much in this company; had probably given too much in any company in work of this kind. But her lack of inhibitions probably encouraged the rest of the cast to let their hair down. Paul Vickerman, playing her son, always had one on tenterhooks. I'd cut his early long speeches to the bone so that he could ease himself gradually into the play, but he constantly gave the impression that he might not last out to the end of even a short speech. Still, the very tentativeness gave his Constantin a persona by no means out of place. Mary Gow as Nina, the girl Constantin loves, also raised doubts as to whether she would last out. If she did, her air of recent grief would come into its own in the last Act. At the moment it was implausible that she should be ambitious to go on the stage, even though the outcome was to be failure.

From the estate manager, Mr Charley, and his wife, Heather Stogden, there was nothing fancy, not even from the former. The latter's love-object, Dr Dorn, was portrayed so well by Mr Chiswell that he must surely have had amateur experience, however far in the past, probably in school plays. When it came to the bits of song he had to sing, his voice went up in pitch, a subtle parody of Mr Charley's habit in actuality, doubtless done mainly for my benefit, remembering our conversation by the lake.

Even the worst performance imaginable of a master-work throws fresh light on it. In professional productions, the Gertrude–Hamlet relation of Arkadin and Constantin, underlined by the playwright, often seems obvious, even boring – though that is too strong a word to use about any part of Chekhov. Lorna Cochrane and Paul Vickerman seemed merely to be moving towards some revelation of it, withheld until a later turn of the drama. It was rather the same with the

contrast between Arkadin's assured theatrical professionalism, and Constantin's experimental essay at
play-writing. As the words were spoken in the White
Drawing-room there was nothing in the least pat or
received about the situation disclosed.

But most striking of all, the opening (which is all
Chekhov gives us) of Constantin's 'play within a play'
had point and merit far beyond anything I'd thought
before – that is, that it was merely an exercise (not
altogether successful) by Chekhov to show a decadent
way of writing; as Madam Arkadin says, a pretension
to 'new forms, a new era in art'. Now it seemed a
prophecy of the 'nuclear winter', the dread of which
would have obsessed the fictional Constantin as much
as the real-life Paul. And once again the lake of reality
played a role.

The stage-direction instructs Constantin to speak his
little prologue in a loud voice. Paul was unable or
unwilling to follow this, but his rather halting style did
not too badly:

> O ancient, honoured shades that nightly haunt this
> lake, close our eyes in sleep that we may see in our
> dreams what will be, in twice ten thousand years
> from now.

As in the play within a play in *Midsummer Night's
Dream*, the 'superior' characters comment scathingly
on this. Sorin says that in twenty thousand years there
won't be anything; Madame Arkadin that given the
audience is asleep (presumably through boredom)
the nothingness can in truth be depicted. Then, on the
temporary stage that has been put up in the park on
Sorin's estate, the curtain rises, revealing Nina sitting
on a rock. Her opening words are:

> Men, lions, eagles, quails, antlered deer, geese,
> spiders, dumb fish and starfish from the sea,

creatures invisible to the eye – in a word, life, all life, has died out at last, having accomplished its melancholy cycle. It is thousands of years since a single living thing was seen on earth, and the sad moon lights her lantern in vain. In the fields, no longer do the storks waken with a cry, nor are the cicadas heard in the lime groves. All is cold, cold, cold!

It is a long speech, but out of mercy to Mary Gow and the forthcoming audience I cut the bulk of it, retaining only enough to make it clear that Nina speaks in the character of the spirit of the universe, in combat with the devil, the source of matter, whose red-eyed appearance and contrived sulphurous smell is received with such further lack of sympathy by the audience that Constantin, in a rage, calls the performance off.

As for the drama's relevance to the private lives of the performers, the actual reading revealed connections that had simply not occurred to me when looking the play through. At the end of the Act, the doctor snatches Masha's snuff-box from her and throws it into the bushes, an extreme but not implausible parallel to medical action at Stares, if not by the gradualist Stembridge, possibly by Dr Singh or the new man, Pentecost. The doctor's brief curtain speech actually begins: 'How nervous you all are! And how much love there is round this enchanted lake!'

Well, the nerves were certain, the love perhaps less so. For some, love had turned to mourning, insomnia, disembodied fantasy.

Afterwards, I found myself leaving the room with Maida Brown. She looked at me from under her ragged fringe of hair, and quoted from the play: 'He's a celebrity but he has a simple heart.'

The speech was by Madame Arkadin about her

novelist-lover, Trigorin, the character played by me.

'That is a statement I don't believe,' said Maida.

She undoubtedly had the power to provoke, even in her lightest remark. For a moment I considered referring maliciously to her being deprived of her 'snuff-box', but laughed instead, and said: 'Come and have a tomato juice. Or carrot juice, if you prefer.' The implication was that she would prefer something stronger. There was in fact a bar set up in a corner of the hall before lunch and dinner where quite a few gathered to sip harmless liquids, doubtless nostalgic for days when their cups inebriated.

'Well, what do you think of your troop of half-wits?' she enquired when I brought the drinks to a seat in one of the deep window embrasures.

'Some of us are wandering in our wits, but I don't think we've lost them.'

'I worked with a team I regarded as dim. Then it turned out that it was I who blew the job. The team stayed on. One of them even took my place. That's what brought me here. That, and one or two other biffs in the vitals.'

'What was the job?'

'Advertising. What else?' She swigged her tomato juice, which coloured the hair on her upper lip, too light really to be dubbed a moustache. 'What other jobs are there these days where you get the bullet for creative failure? PR perhaps. A worse fate.'

'The theatre isn't kind to non-success.'

'Oh I don't know. People seem to bumble along there year after year, as in most jobs.'

I couldn't help, as I looked at her, imagining her as Fred Boraston's lost daughter, utterly impossible as the coincidence might be. 'Speaking of our wits and of our being here, Lorna Cochrane ascribes many breakdowns to being orphaned.'

'Orphaned?' broke in Maida, as though the word did not exist.

I said: 'At its simplest the thing works like this. An adult suffers a bereavement – the death of a spouse or an offspring – and that revives the devastating sense of loss suffered by that adult as a child when his mother or father – or both – died. So there is really a double – or treble – loss, and the adult fails to cope with the anxiety and pain and depression that can't wholly be accounted for.' I was half hoping Maida might volunteer some information about her childhood, possible orphaned status, and so forth, but nothing emerged except a watchful eye. 'Naturally, the thing can be exacerbated if the orphaned state in childhood was especially unhappy – the child being institutionalized or the family becoming penurious.'

'There were far more orphans in Victorian times than now,' said Maida at last. 'Do you thing there was a greater incidence of neurosis?'

Her tone, as usual, was not friendly. If in her work she had been always on the *qui vive* to argue, even pick a quarrel, no wonder they got shot of her in the end. Mr Boraston's word had not been too strong: she was 'daunting'. I was too cowardly to risk some rebuff by probing further about her past.

'I daresay. Though we do our best to counter the improvement in the expectation of life by increasing the number of one-parent families.'

'Very good.'

She seemed so genuinely struck by my remark that I was encouraged to respond at last to her opening move. 'I'm not a celebrity, and I believe I have a simple heart.'

'Nonsense. Everyone here knows about you. And yet can't fathom you.'

The latter statement was not unfamiliar: the

headmaster of my dream had even written something of the kind in my school report. 'The whiskers make me mysterious. Clean-shaven I'm quite different,' I said. But why was I ever considered enigmatic? I remembered Sammy telling me as much when the barriers were eventually down after our first encounter.

She ignored the facetiousness. 'Who's the little fellow who plays the doctor?' she asked.

'He's called Chiswell. I believe his first name is Hilary. Very nice man. And he's a widower,' I added, hoping to tease her.

'He spoke his lines nicely,' said Maida, ignoring my last remark. Her compliment was unexpected. She quoted from the play again: ' "Only the serious is beautiful." Do you believe that?'

'Well I don't –' The summons to lunch sounded. 'Saved by the gong,' I said, when the reverberations had died away. 'There's no doubt we're all serious here. But what that signifies . . .'

'Yes,' she said, 'being bonkers is a serious matter.'

As we got up to go into the dining-room, I said: 'Mr Chiswell was at Istanbul Airport when the commandos went in.'

'Hell fire!'

'What happened to him, I don't know.'

Some actually passed into the dining-room before the gong sounded, presumably less through hunger than boredom. The result was Denise separated me from Maida, not to my displeasure; she was no ideal luncheon companion.

15

TEA was another 'help yourself' meal. Plates of
biscuits and large tea-pots were placed on the bar-
counter in the hall, a labour-saving and rather stingy
arrangement presumably deplored by Fred Boraston. I
debated whether or not to partake of its meagre
gastronomic rewards, but between lunch and dinner
was a considerable interval, not entirely filled by the
therapeutic recreations provided, and I went in. I had
forgotten Mrs Cochrane's admonition to put myself
with her and her visiting sister until I saw her and a
stranger in the embrasure I'd occupied with Maida
before lunch. I felt an obligation to take my tea and
digestive biscuit over to them. Mrs Cochrane introduced me to a younger but stouter and coarser version
of herself, Mrs Doggett. 'This is Mr Toyne, Alice, the
actor I mentioned to you,' she said. I was immediately
conscious that my interruption, however pleasing to
Mrs Cochrane, was not to the taste of her sister – who
even made some attempt to continue the dialogue they
had been having before my arrival. Almost as
immediately came the sense of Mrs Cochrane as the
oppressed, Mrs Doggett the oppressor, though in
isolation the former had scarcely shown herself with a
weak persona. It was also evident that Mrs Doggett
was not a teacher of elocution. One speculated on the
aptness or otherwise of names, as implied by Heather
Stogden. The Lorna character had married the
nicely-named Cochrane; the Alice character the

nastily-named Doggett. Luckily, for my unease, I felt I need not linger, since there was no room on the window-seat and no chair to draw up to it – such chairs as there were being by the centre table, of theatrical-gigantesque style, probably part of the original furnishings.

'Are you staying in the village?' I enquired of Mrs Doggett, to make a little conversation to lessen the guilt of my departing.

'I am.'

'Several houses take in guests, as well as the pub,' said Mrs Cochrane.

The neurotic have given rise to a cottage industry, I thought, but refrained from uttering. 'I expect we shall meet again,' I said, preparing my exit line. 'Are you staying for the play-reading?' At once I realized I'd said too much, encouraging Mrs Doggett's sojourn, letting Mrs Cochrane down.

'I don't know anything about it.'

'Well, goodbye for the time being, anyway.' Make your exits neat and decisive, old Frank Faulkland used to say when I was with him in rep in prehistoric days. I did my best to follow the advice now.

Through the open double-doors of the Red Drawing-room I saw Mr Chiswell sitting alone, and took my second cup of tea and biscuit to join him.

'Were we passable this morning?' he asked. 'Or worse than you expected?'

I reassured him.

'I'd forgotten,' he said, 'how much there is about the theatre in *The Seagull*. What does the Mr Charley character say? "The stage has degenerated, Irina Nicolaievna". Then I say something like: "It's true that in these times there aren't many outstanding talents, but the average actor has much improved". Do you think that may be true now? I feel I was extremely lucky myself to see great days – Gielgud, Richardson and Olivier at the New, Burton at the Old Vic.'

'All days are great. One just gets older.'

'Is that it?'

'When I first joined the profession, everyone off-stage did Robert Atkins anecdotes in Robert Atkins impersonations. Now everyone does Gielgud. Before Atkins it was probably Benson, and before Benson, Irving.'

'Yes, but is that sort of chap still arriving on the scene? So many actors now seem to have small-range, lower middle-class voices, all suited to the kind of play you get on television. I say, you'll think me an awful snob.'

I laughed and said: 'Mrs Brown told me she thought you at least spoke your lines well.'

He looked pleased. 'Is that the Masha?'

'Yes. Perhaps she has her eye on you. I don't think she possesses a husband at the moment.'

'Even if I were twenty years younger I wouldn't much like to be captured by her.'

'Nevertheless, this place must have led to some unlikely romances.'

He glanced at his watch. 'You'll have to excuse me. I must keep my date with Stembridge.'

'How do you get on with him?'

'All right. He doesn't seem to do or say much, but I'm better than when I came here.' He looked away. 'Perhaps I couldn't have got worse.'

'Stembridge supplies the obvious, the commonplace element in life, lacking in most of us, I suppose.'

'Yes,' said Chiswell. 'Think of his fountain-pen.'

The penny didn't drop.

'Bigger, fatter, than any possessed by his patients.'

I laughed. 'That's how he imposes on us, is it?'

'In the Stembridge world everything stands for

something else. I leave you with that profound thought.'

In the early evening I heard on my transistor in the bedroom of the assassination of the President. In a way, it was merely one more incident in the current series of Middle East disasters, an horrific scenario that had even obtruded itself into Paul Vickerman's *curriculum vitae*. Not for the first time one thought of the nuclear powers being drawn into the conflicts, and a train of events ending with Constantin's extinguishment of all lives' sad cycle. I wondered if Paul possessed a transistor. In any case, despite the limitations on the set in the Red Drawing-room, he would eventually catch up with the news on TV. The disorder in the world was worse than the disorder in Stares. In fact, the element of fantasy here seemed to hold at bay the world's ugly realities – Mrs Cochrane's Oedipus son Paul, Boraston's Perdita daughter Maida, Dr Mowle as Viennese Duke: the very irresolution of these situations made time appear to stand still. Should we all eventually go out into the reality of religious and nation-state maniacs, or retreat further into the asylums of the wholly potty?

I was proceeding along the corridor from my bedroom with the vague notion of a pre-prandial juice in the hall bar when I encountered Mrs Cochrane coming out of her room. 'Are you drying out?' she asked.

I hesitated, wondering what was in store. 'No.'

She took the few steps back to the door of her room, and opened it. 'Come in and have a drink. Take a comfortable chair.'

The room was bigger than mine. Dusk was at the windows, some perfume lingered in the air. She produced from the wardrobe a bottle of Johnnie Walker, its familiar slender, angular form unfamiliar in these surroundings. 'No ice, and only tap water, available, I'm afraid.'

'Branch, as I think the Americans say, will be OK.'

She dispensed a generous measure of scotch in each recognizable Stares tooth-glass. 'Of course, you must think I'm a secret drinker, foolishly breaking instructions.'

'Well, I certainly didn't expect more than carrot juice this evening.'

'I've stopped drinking by myself but I needed consolation. Are you sure you're not here to dry out? I wouldn't want to lead you into temptation.'

'Booze is not my problem,' I said, wondering whether in fact it had fundamentally been Sammy's.

'Better health,' she said, raising her glass slightly.

'Same to you.'

'My old man of the sea is waiting downstairs.'

For a moment I envisaged persecution by Mr Charley, or even that some ancient, unwelcome admirer had turned up. After all, despite her stick, Mrs Cochrane was not utterly an emotional has-been.

'My sister Alice,' she said venomously.

'Oh.'

'She looks not unlike a man, too.'

It was true: Mrs Doggett had more than a touch of the pantomime dame. 'She's stopping for dinner, then?' It wasn't easy to hit on what to say.

'Yes. And for how many more dinners, God alone knows. I wish they would put their feet down against any kind of visiting. Look at the effect on Mary Gow. I daresay if Dr Mowle were on the spot things would be less lenient. Of course, I expect you're wondering how Alice will get back to her digs in the village. She doesn't drive, I may explain, so I shall have to order a car for her. First there's the evening to get through. I must say I appreciated your coming over at tea-time. In the circumstances it didn't relieve the situation, but I suppose it was outrageous of me to think I could unload some of my burden on you.'

The Sindbad imagery persisted. And Mrs Cochrane's speech was quite unlike her usual style. 'Can I do anything tonight? I feel I let you down at tea-time, but . . .'

'I shan't impose on you,' she said grandly, and hoisted herself with her stick, and poured me another scotch.

'I must temper this,' I said, and went to the wash-basin. On the dressing-table were propped several gouaches on paper, presumably executed by Mrs Cochrane in Noel Mummery's art sessions. Her subconscious seemed to consist of rather balloon-like landscapes and cloudscapes, not without effect.

When I returned to the easy chair, she said quite simply: 'I can't get rid of her. I don't mean just here, but at home. After her husband died she became homeless, so what could I do but take her in, temporarily, as I thought? He'd had a so-called antique shop and they lived over it as tenants. Archie Doggett died insolvent, as near as makes no difference. Of course, Alice and I don't get on, never have got on. There's nothing so wearing as the antagonism of sisters, usually thrown close together because of their mainly domestic lives. She's obviously hanging on till I pass on, then hoping to inherit. What can I do? Sue her for possession of her bedroom? Persuade the police to throw her out? I'm sure if it weren't for her I wouldn't be here.'

I saw the long Arnold Bennettesque perspectives of their lives, the close parallels diverging in early womanhood, only to return in old age. 'Can you be firm?' I said inadequately.

'I'm as firm as I can be,' said Lorna Cochrane. 'But she has the hide of an elephant. Of course, she grudges

—100—

the money I spend here, though it's my money. She thinks of it already as hers. She herself would never spend money on anyone else. She never bought family birthday presents. Can you imagine that? A real Scrooge.'

'I *am* sorry.'

'What is it the doctor says at the end of Act I? "How much love . . ." '

'What an amount of love round this enchanted lake.'

'That's it. You've an actor's memory.'

'I thought myself of the aptness of the phrase to Stares.'

'Yes,' said Mrs Cochrane, 'but concern about money, greed for it, can easily take over from love.'

I thought of Sammy. Perhaps the rewards of my success, as well as success itself, had soured, had galled him. 'I suppose it's only when you have it that you can underestimate money's power.' There was no doubt that the tendency to make such pronouncements was increased by the well-being creeping over me from the sipping of the Johnnie Walker, a sensation I had forgotten, of insidious attraction. The world of tedious chores and characters, of a null future, was slipping away.

'That's enough of my troubles for the time being,' said Mrs Cochrane. 'Now what about the play? Shall we all have sufficient stamina to bring it off?'

We talked about the cast for a few moments, and then she said: 'How cruel Madame Arkadin is to her son! I hope Paul doesn't think the worse of me for speaking her words.'

'I'm sure he can distinguish art from reality.'

'I wonder. Perhaps his own mother teases and denigrates him in the same way. I wouldn't want him to put me in that class.'

As I was thinking how odd it was for Mrs Cochrane

to assume in the next breath the truth of a speculation she had herself enunciated, I saw the door slowly open. The locks on the bedroom doors were not automatic: to ensure security the key had to be used. Into the aperture came a face that at first I did not recognize, perhaps expecting a chambermaid, then saw it belonged to Mrs Doggett. She saw me, the head half withdrew, then re-emerged, with the rest of the substantial body. This slight pantomine was not observed by Mrs Cochrane from her upright chair by the table in the window, though a sound must have alerted her, for she turned her head even as Mrs Doggett spoke.

'Oh Lorna, I thought you would be alone. I'd no idea . . .' The somewhat common voice, for this speech at any rate, was not at all what the Widow Twanky features promised, being extremely ingratiating, doubtless for my benefit, though the unfinished sentence contained an implication that improper behaviour of some kind had been taking place, or was about to.

Mrs Cochrane was furious, yet her voice trembled so much it gave the impression of weakness, already yielding the field to her sister, however clearly the latter was in the wrong. 'How on earth did you get up here?'

'They told me your room number at the desk. You'd been so long, Lorna. I was beginning to worry about you. You know how you've been lately. I thought perhaps you'd . . .' Again extreme happenings were left unexpressed.

'Why didn't you knock?' But I thought Mrs Cochrane's enquiry rather gave ground, and was possibly put in for my benefit – as though showing that she at least of the family was aware of social proprieties.

'I wasn't absolutely sure you'd still be in your room, Lorna. You might have been in the garden, by the lake . . .'

I wondered if Mrs Doggett held in reserve some suicidal threat, or even attempt, by her sister.

'Well, please leave us and go downstairs. I'll collect you at dinner-time, if not before. Go and sit in the television room. You can ask at the desk where that is.' One could see that the irony was wasted on Mrs Doggett. The Bennettesque divergence of the sisters' lives had resulted in the one acquiring along the way a culture altogether subtler, more vulnerable than the other's – which had probably changed not at all from that of her parents, a culture quite ignoring books, plays, the niceties of speech, *comme il faut* in general.

Mrs Doggett had the last word. 'I'm sorry if I've intruded – Mr Twain, isn't it? – as you've heard, I'd no idea . . .' She backed out.

'My God,' said Lorna Cochrane, a strong expletive for her, so I judged. 'I'm sorry, too, but really sorry.'

'You mustn't think anything of it.'

'I'll never sleep tonight thinking of nothing else.'

'Come on, Lorna. Cheer up. It wasn't the end of the world. And remember, you'll soon be ordering that car to take her away.' I was conscious of using her forename for the first time. Perhaps she was, also, for she reached across and tapped me on the knee with her stick.

'You must have another drink after that. Will you pour it?'

'Only if you'll join me.' I imagined her going back home, after what alleviation Stares had been able to confer, and finding Alice Doggett in her drawing-room, her kitchen, snoring in a bedroom. Sometimes the worst human troubles were slightly comic clichés, like mothers-in-law and nagging wives. And I thought:

I had a nagging wife, taken to the extreme degree.

I righteously intended to sit with the sisters at dinner, but Denise had other ideas. She showed me to a table for two at which a young man was already sitting, not previously seen. She introduced him to me as 'Mr Waddilove'. When she had gone, he said: 'My first name's David.'

'Mine's Bill.' It turned out that he was indeed a newcomer to Stares, and that this was his first meal. Was Denise a remote tentacle of Stares' therapy, deliberately ensuring my propinquity to this very personable youngster? Or, more likely, not therapy but a continuance of the supply of patients, since the amatory so often led to the melancholy. There came back the beginning of a certain new term at school, my announcing I was going to look the new boys over, and returning saying with covert pleasure: 'One of them is exactly like me.' It was true: he had the same shaped head, a similar nose. But why that should excite me wasn't – isn't – easy to explain. His name was Chadwin. Quite soon he drifted from notice, being younger, dumber than I'd imagined, and placed in a lower form. And in those days I didn't realize the nature of my nature.

David Waddilove knew or had been told of my profession. We were led on from that to the play-reading. 'There's a part still going – a character who only has a few lines. I thought I would bring the chap taking it in more by letting him also read the stage directions. What d'you say? Will you have a go? I hope so.'

'The truth is,' he said, 'I don't want to do anything.'

He had ordered the fish pie, but only shuffled it about his plate. I'd put that down to an injudicious choice (which indeed I might have warned him about), for the fish was not always of the freshest, made-up dishes being especially suspect. But his words – the first indication that his place was really in Stares and not an hotel suited to a travelling up-and-coming young executive – prompted me to notice, even in the dim light, his pallor, dark eye-sockets. I said: 'You won't be alone in this place with that feeling. Even among the cast.' I left the question of his participation with him, to think about, and we went on (in the typical manner of new recruits and old hands) to talk about times and routines, recreational facilities and institutional characters.

That evening produced another image that stayed with me. Much later, passing the open door of the television room, I saw, among others, Paul Vickerman in the darkness, illuminated by the screen, which showed a crowd of white-garbed figures shaking their fists, no doubt one side or the other involved with the assassination. At that hour the programme was probably one of lengthy analysis, usually judged to be harmless. In Paul's case, the maniacs of the Middle East were even closer to his life than to the lives of the rest of us. I thought that the long opening speech in Constantin's play could well have appeared in Paul's *curriculum vitae*: 'The bodies of all living things have turned to dust, and been transformed into stones and water and clouds . . .'

16

DAVID Waddilove's words came back to me as I rose the next morning after a whitish night, facing the read-through of Act II. All at once the play-reading seemed ludicrous, undertaken for no other reason than my self-aggrandizement in an ambience where such served only to emphasize unbalance.

I'd been speculating in the night about David's surname. Had it anything to do with love, or was the final syllable merely like the Russian 'ov' or 'off', as in the forename of the character I'd asked him to play? 'Waddi' was even more mysterious, though there had been a boy at school with the still stranger name of Waddicor. Possibly Waddilove and Waddicor were obscure villages in the north. By no means for the first time, Stares struck me as a microcosm of England, not least in its assembly of local accents and allegiances, and notwithstanding – indeed, some might argue because of – the qualification of neurosis. What was the phrase? 'This country of ours where no one is well.'

David was not among the cast who assembled after breakfast in the White Drawing-room, but Yakov does not appear in Act II anyway. As the play proceeded I was surprised once more at its occasional aptness to the real life characters and situations of the actors, though I'd sometimes observed this in professional productions of serious drama, whether due to inspired casting or the dramatist's power to embody universal actions and personae, who knows? There was also the factor of even the amateur player bending his lines to his own characteristics. In the trialogue at the start of the Act between Madame Arkadin, Masha and the doctor, only the first named had words that didn't fit, her liveliness not consorting well with the still-threatening presence of Mrs Doggett. But even here her remarks about keeping herself up to the mark in dress and grooming were borne out in actuality. Masha's first speech seemed an accurate parody of her normal manner: 'And *I* feel as though I was born a thousand years ago . . . very often I've absolutely no desire to go on living. Of course, that's ridiculous. One ought to pull oneself together and shake all that off.' The resolute turn to her words was rightly unconvincing. When, as the doctor, he came to the snatch of song he has to sing, translated as 'Tell her, O flowers . . .' and no doubt something that was familiar to the Russian audience of the day, Mr Chiswell substituted the start of Don José's post-prison aria from *Carmen* in what was obviously an ancient English translation. 'See here thy floweret treasured well . . .' It was a real *coup de théâtre*.

There were some wonderful accidental conjunctions in another little trialogue that follows Boraston/Sorin's dropping off in his chair. 'Pleasant dreams!' says the doctor ironically. Madame Arkadin wakes her brother up by calling out his name, then accuses him of being asleep. 'Not a bit of it', says Sorin.

MADAME ARKADIN: You won't take medical advice, that's what's wrong.
SORIN: I'd be happy to take it, but the doctor here won't give me any.
DOCTOR DORN: Taking medical advice at sixty?
SORIN: Even at sixty one wants to live.

Naturally one had to add fifteen or so years for the

increased expectation of life. I wondered if Fred Boraston found encouragement in Sorin's desire. Certainly in the ensuing dialogue he would see confirmation of his scepticism about Stares:

DOCTOR DORN: Well, take some valerian drops.
MADAME ARKADIN: I think it might do him good to go to some seaside resort.
DOCTOR DORN: Yes, it might. Or it might not.
MADAME ARKADIN: I really can't make you out.
DOCTOR DORN: There's nothing *to* make out. It's all perfectly clear.

As the ensuing business proceeded about Sorin's needing to give up smoking, and alcohol and tobacco destroying the ego and making one think of oneself in the third person, culminating with Maida saying it's lunch-time and that her foot's gone to sleep, and hobbling away to the doctor's comment that she's going to throw back a couple of drinks before lunch, the text was almost embarrassingly apropos. But the readers ploughed through it, seemingly not turning a hair, Mr Boraston telling of his twenty-eight years in the law without ever having lived –'I want to live', in Sorin's famous phrase.

What a marvellous work of art it was, I saw all over again as the dramatist repeated his motifs (so often with a comic effect enhancing the insight into reality) broadly enough for the audience to pick them up, yet without any vulgarity – like the motifs of a great but popular symphonic melodist. When Nina later reports that after the row about the non-availability of carriage-horses Madame Arkadin is weeping and Sorin has an attack of asthma, and the doctor says: 'I'll go and give them both some valerian drops', I thought of the opportunity the line gave to an actor who would speak it not wholly ironically.

And yet, of course, reality had a seriousness art could never equal, as Chekhov himself was perfectly aware, not least in the moment when he has Trigorin make notes in his pocket-book about Masha: 'Takes snuff and drinks vodka . . . Always black. The school-master is in love with her . . .' Yes, we think, and this is how she is depicted in the play, but the very picking out of the obvious characteristics at once gives Masha extra dimensions. I'd severely cut Trigorin's long speeches partly to shorten the performance, partly to disemphasize myself. Included in the cuts were Trigorin's lines about his fear of being carried off to a lunatic asylum by his acquaintances, whose praise is a mere deception, the deception of a person who is mortally ill. I also omitted much of what Trigorin says to Nina about young girls – that he doesn't often meet them, those who are young and interesting, and so in his fiction they are untrue to life – though naturally the irony had to be retained of his saying that it was therefore a pity that since he was going away that day he and Nina would be hardly likely to meet again. For of course the play turns on Nina eventually being 'ruined' by her subsequent association with Trigorin.

Despite my omissions, I looked afresh at Nina/ Mary Gow: at the tangled hair, shining with youth none the less; the lip 'as though a bee had stung it'; the general air of – was it? – incompetence, playing life like the game of bridge she was so bad at. However, she got through her lines all right: along the way com-petent school mistresses had prevailed upon her to come up to scratch in required activities. I suppose it was as true of me as of Trigorin that I'd forgotten or, rather, couldn't picture to myself how girls felt at eighteen or nineteen. I remember what an actress friend had years ago said to me about the interests of her daughter –'only boys and clothes'– and thinking they were also my own. But that concerned a girl of fifteen: it took only a year or two for complications to develop – rebellion, anorexia, addiction of various kinds, sexual distaste or promiscuity.

It is in Act II that Chekhov introduces the eponymous seagull – shot by Constantin, laid by him at Nina's feet, and picked up by her, for she, anyway, is not a character to shirk experience. Perhaps the bird has always seemed a not altogether satisfactory symbol, being to a certain degree at once obvious and far fetched, but there is no doubt that the episode is extremely telling where Trigorin jots down another entry in his pocket-book, is questioned by Nina as to what he is writing and tells her: 'I'm just making a note . . . only an idea that occurred to me, an idea for a short story. A young girl has grown up on the shores of a lake, like you. She loves the lake, like a seagull; and like a seagull she's free and happy. But a man comes along by chance, and having nothing better to do, destroys her, like this seagull here.' It is one of those outrageous double bluffs that audiences accept, even delight in, and which playwrights are so fond of, even Shakespeare.

I retained Trigorin's words about success, which Nina accuses him of being spoilt by. I wondered whether Trigorin was being honest in his riposte, when he says that he's never liked himself as a writer. Even with my limited experience I knew the feeling only too well, yet optimism about one's work is constantly renewed. Much more believable are Trigorin's remarks about the impossibility of bringing truthfully into his work the people, their sufferings and future; science and the rights of man – so that in the end all he feels good for is to depict landscapes.

We broke up early: too many of the readers had clinical appointments for us to carry on, but luckily Act II is short. I left the White Drawing-room with

Mr Chiswell. 'You made me smile with your *Carmen* warbling,' I said.

'Well,' he said, 'I wondered if it wasn't too much like Mr Charley.'

'Oh, I don't think grand opera is in his repertoire.'

'Perhaps not, but he was apparently, so he says, near to being in a prison cell where a floweret's odour might have cheered him.'

In the exodus I lost Hilary Chiswell, and found Mr Charley bobbing along at my side. Had he heard my exchange with the former? For a moment or two I was uneasy, but almost immediately he said in his normal manner: 'I don't think I ever told you that to add insult to injury I was bloody well burgled the day I attended court. French windows wrecked and all sorts of treasures gone.'

'Awful.' But perhaps there was poetic justice in it, since he himself had been trying to lay his hands on a treasure. And it might have been that though he had not overheard Mr Chiswell's remarks, the sight of the Dr Dorn character started melodic connections in his mind. As we went towards the hall down the long corridor (whose windows disclosed some strollers on the terrace), he sang, *sotto voce* but in his usual falsetto:

> Sometimes between long shadows on the grass
> The little truant waves of sunlight pass.
> My eyes grow dim with tenderness the while,
> Thinking I see thee, thinking I see thee smile.

Though the sun was at its noon height, the season caused the shadows of the perambulators on the terrace to be noticeably cast, no doubt prompting, if subconsciously, the choice of Mr Charley's *chanson*. I thought that his repertoire, already outmoded, might possibly he handed down through a purely aural tradition, but the meaning – the celebration of romantic love – utterly lost in a degenerate, sexually uninhibited culture.

In his normal register, Mr Charley said: 'I've got to go off and see Stembridge now, so *adieu.*' As I entered the hall I found Maida Brown had taken his place.

'Is it twenty-four hours ago that we had a pre-lunch juice together?' she said.

'Time's said to drag here, but in fact it goes like lightning.'

'It's the monotonous routine,' she said. 'Can you bear to juice again with me?'

Even her social pleasantries had an acerbic undertone, 'I'll make the effort.'

'The chit must be down to me today,' she said, as we approached the bar, which was just being set up.

The word led me to speculate that she might have had a rackety past in an Eastern land – perhaps where the President had just been knocked off – in which the British lived their social life in clubs.

We moved away from the little bar with our variously coloured drinks. She said: 'I say, this play is getting close to life. Did you choose it on purpose?'

'Hadn't the least notion of its striking home in any particular.'

'What about the casting?'

'Well, even there it was mainly opportunist.'

'Is it supposed to do us good to act out these fictional aliases?'

'I've no idea. I suggested the play-reading to Noel for general amusement, my own not least.'

'Shall we let history repeat itself and sit in the window seat over there?'

'OK.'

The sunlight filtered in as before. Maida said: 'I expect you think I look one hell of a mess.' Before I could find a reply, she added: 'Let me tell you I looked a hundred times worse a month ago.'

'I shouldn't think anyone here looks at their best.'

'I'm going to reform.' She directed her usual look of defiance, now curiously at odds with her words. 'Sounds naive, but there it is. I'm going to give up – the booze, smoking, uppers, downers.'

'Quite a shipping order.'

'And sex. I'm weary of being unrequitedly smitten on Constantin Gavrilovich.'

'I take it you mean a generic character rather than Paul Vickerman.'

'I'm leaving Paul to Lorna Cochrane.'

'She's maternal about him, as in the play.'

'Maternal, shmaternal – who cares, so long as a mother loves her son? Mind you, I could do with a fag right now. To say nothing of other pleasures.' Her renunciation of cigarettes was recent, for her right first finger was still brown, the colour extending up the long narrow nail. 'And on the positive side, I'm going to get a job, and a place to live. I'm sick of bumming around other people's flats and houses. Besides, what the hell's going to happen to me when I get too old to work? I want a job where you contribute to a pension. I'm not too old for that.' She laughed. 'I want all the things I used to disdain.'

'Perhaps you'll marry again,' I said, thinking of Mr Chiswell, and chancing my arm as to her exact marital state.

'Not on your nelly.'

At that moment I saw Mrs Doggett enter the hall, a questing look on her heavy features. Seeing me, she came straight over. What could she want?

'I'm very sorry indeed to trouble you, Mr Twain, but I'm looking for my sister. She said she was doing the play this morning, but they say that's over. She's not in her room and I wondered if you knew where she'd got to.' The truculence under the fawning tone was familiar from the bedroom scene of yesterday.

'She may have taken a stroll.'

'I've looked in the garden. She wouldn't have gone far, it's quite near a meal-time.'

Mrs Doggett showed no sign of moving away, so I introduced her to Maida, who said: 'I ought to be introducing you. This is Mr Toyne not Twain.'

Mrs Doggett was not abashed. 'Pardon. My sister couldn't have spoken clearly.'

A demon seized me. 'Well, I'm going into the garden, perhaps as far as the park. If I see her I'll tell her you are looking for her.' I rose, and left them together. I should have liked to be a fly on the wall during the ensuing exchanges between the pair, though probably Maida followed suit and simply walked away.

In the garden the geraniums and michaelmas daisies were still vivid. The starlings in their autumnal speckles whooped in the trees with a dying fall, and a few busied themselves on the lawn, hunchback figures, hands in pockets, as it were. I approached a (or the) gardener, a figure I had observed before: himself not unbird-like – diminutive, small head, prominent nose and chin made more prominent through the pretty well complete absence of teeth, possibly habitual, false teeth being spurned. I came so close to him that a word seemed called for. He was removing some sproutings from the trunk of a tree whose boughs bore leaves already golden, as well as a sprinkling of white blossom in which bees were foraging.

'Marvellous tree. What's it called?'

He paused in his snipping. *Prunus subhirtella autumnalis*. In this weather you gets the blossom while the majority of the leaves has still not been blown down.'

'Marvellous.'

'Aye, it's a nice little tree. I likes to keep it tidy.' He snapped his secateurs. 'Always carry your seekatewers about with you. That's the golden rule. And a nice sharp penknife.'

'Afraid I'm no gardener.'

He pushed his cloth-cap farther up his brow, revealing fresh hollows in his tiny physiognomy. Over the years the gesture had imprinted itself on the cap as an area of incredible greasiness. 'Keeping these grounds nice is good for those here, is what I always says.'

'Yes, I can see that.' It was another strand of Stares' modest therapy.

'Some on 'em needs it. I've come across some rum'uns, believe you me.'

'I suppose you have.'

'I have that. Even the ladies. There's some rum things been said to me, just passing, like you, sir.'

'I'd better pass on.'

The gardener laughed, his gums so shrunken they failed to reveal themselves. I went through the gateway in the garden wall – the gates permanently open during the day – into the parkland. There were conkers shining underfoot. Few inmates had ventured at this hour as far as the lake, so it was with a real sense of discovery that in the distance I saw Mrs Cochrane come round a boathouse affair on the lake's margin. I kept steadily on my way so that she wouldn't think I'd come searching for her. From some distance she waved her stick in greeting. We met on the narrow path. I said: 'I think I've gone far enough. Can I walk back with you?'

'Of course,' she said, the phrase appropriate for once.

We exchanged some words about the miraculous

continuance of the warm sunlight, and then I said: 'Your sister has been looking for you.'

'She spoke to you, then?'

I related the circumstances, including my unloading of her on Maida, which I thought might amuse her. The news seemed to stop her in her tracks. 'Oh, I hope Maida behaves herself.'

'I should think she would soon leave your sister in the lurch.' I wasn't at all sure what Mrs Cochrane's words signified.

'I hope so.'

Perhaps Mrs Cochrane was ashamed of Mrs Doggett's speech and general behaviour. We had halted near the seat where Mr Boraston and I had discussed *Mansfield Park* and he had lifted the veil a little on his private life. Mrs Cochrane said: 'Can you spare me a few minutes if we sit down?'

It appeared an inevitable turn to events when we were side by side, and she said: 'I want to tell you what precipitated my coming here.' The long word seemed to indicate a premeditated confession, not necessarily to me. 'I'd rather you learned it from me than from Alice, or via Maida. It's a thing that has ruined my life in the locality, laid me open more than ever to Alice's impositions. I was found guilty in the magistrates' court of shop-lifting.'

'How rotten!' The words failed to express my shocked sense of the frustrations of elderly women, and, so familiar from my youth, the strict *mores* of a respectable bourgeois community.

'I dread going back home. In theory I could sell up, move somewhere else. In fact, the size of the house is one of Alice's arguments for moving in permanently. But I lived there so long with my husband . . .' Her voice gave out at last.

'I doubt your sister would have the opportunity to

say much to Maida Brown. In any case, Maida would take it in her stride, not bother to pass anything on.'

'Naturally, you assume I was guilty.'

I made some sort of noise.

'Of course, the strange thing is,' she said, 'I now wonder whether I was guilty.' She paused for a moment, and I remembered Mr Charley speculating about his guilt. Then she continued: 'My wonderful daily woman shops for me, but she was ill and I went to the supermarket myself. Three items were found in my bag instead of the shop's receptacle. It was there being three that made them bring the case. One, perhaps two, could have been put down to inadvertence. Being stopped outside the store, and all that followed, seemed to draw a curtain on my memory. I believe I've always been too amenable in life. I just went along with everybody's supposition that I was one of those women who late in life take to shop-lifting, the motives ranging from irrational fear of poverty to calling attention to their lonely plight. But what if I just absent-mindedly put the stuff direct into my bag?'

'I can see that as a strong possibility.'

'My solicitor, when he spoke in court in mitigation I think you call it, said I would go for treatment. My doctor had suggested Stares. So here I am.'

A robin descended quite close to us. The breast was preternaturally red: no doubt, like the starlings, its plumage was fresh. 'I appreciate your confidence very much,' I said.

Mrs Cochrane drew a pattern with her stick in the gravel in front of the seat. The robin twirled up into the nearest tree. 'Thinking about it, I daresay I should have come here soon after my husband passed on. I didn't realize how thoroughly my existence had been turned upside down.'

'Would your sister really . . . spread the news?' I

was going to say 'spill the beans', but the colloquialism would have wrongly coloured a situation whose drama required playing of a high degree of seriousness.

'The only thing that would stop her would be the feeling that as my sister her respectability would be damaged by the business getting out. Otherwise, she has no scruples. She's been like that always. Of course, you're too young to remember the days when daughters sometimes were imprisoned in their families until they managed to get married, simply because of the low wages paid to young women – and not so young women. Imagine, I shared a bedroom with Alice for twenty years! And she's still going through my belongings. Yes, while I'm here she'll be looking and fingering and reading in my home. I think of that all the time. Of course, I put a good few things in the bank's custody, and some papers are locked up – though not with great security. It would be quite possible for her to find a key or two to fit, and I wouldn't put it past her to go to any amount of trouble to do that.'

I couldn't help wondering, unprepossessing as I'd found Mrs Doggett, whether Lorna Cochrane wasn't constructing rather an exaggerated monster, then thought of the picture of Sammy I might depict, in his last months. I suppose I'd always been reluctant to assume the existence in real life of evil characters, wanting (through a psychological quirk I couldn't account for) to think the best of people. Presumably Chekhov, unlike Dickens and the Bard, was of similar mind, not believing in villains – unless characters like Trigorin and the doctor in *The Seagull* could be regarded as such, simply through their excess of selfishness. And like some mysterious sound in a Chekhov play, there came faintly from the house, over the garden and down the parterre, a hollow booming – the summons to lunch, which Denise always sounded (while the weather was still clement, anyway) with the great front door open.

'I think that's the gong.' I was glad of something immediate to say not apropos of Mrs Cochrane's confession. I helped her to her feet, and we set off along the path. 'If it's any comfort, you can remember that everyone here has a secret they wouldn't like revealed. They would be understanding about the circumstances of yours, without exception.'

'I feel better, easier, having told you.'

'Good, good.'

The virginia creeper growing over the garden wall was an unlikely red, its final flourish before temporary death.

'It's a sad season,' I said. 'But then in temperate lands perhaps all seasons are sad. Like their music.'

'But Chekhov's sad, too,' said Mrs Cochrane as though she, also, had been prompted to think about *The Seagull*. 'And he lived in a climate of extremes.'

'Life *is* sad.' I wasn't sure whether I believed the cliché or not.

17

'WE rather feel our destinies have become entangled,' said Heather Stogden. She grinned, indicating the essential facetiousness of the remark.

I'd observed her and Hilary Chiswell lunching together, and, carrying my coffee out on to the terrace, fallen in with them.

'Pursued by you, I shouldn't have been so churlish as the doctor,' said Mr Chiswell gallantly. No doubt the difference in their years enabled him to make such a remark without consequences, though it could be that he wished them. If one learns anything from life it is that age and ill-assortment are no bar to amorous entanglement.

We sat at one of the terrace tables. 'We've been speculating about the date of *The Seagull*,' said Mrs Stogden. 'And between us have arrived at 1905.'

'Not all that long before I was born,' said Mr Chiswell, as though thoroughly to defuse his previous remark.

'A good bit earlier, in fact,' I said. '1898.'

'Only two years before *The Interpretation of Dreams*,' said Mr Chiswell.

'And the outbreak of the Boer War and the first performance of the *Enigma Variations*. When I was in the play as a young actor years ago, I researched it. It came the year after the discovery of the electron and a few years before the invention of cellophane.'

'What an amazing epoch!' said Mr Chiswell.

Mrs Stogden asked me what part I'd played. I told her, and added: 'But I understudied the Constantin.'

'Did you ever get to go on?'

'Not once.'

Dr Singh came along the terrace, occasionally stopping for a brief word with those who could not get enough of the really unseasonable warmth and sunlight. I'd been introduced to him early in my stay at Stares, remaining unconvinced of his value, despite his undoubted charisma. He actually took the fourth seat at our table.

'You never come to my seminars,' he said, addressing me. His smile removed some of the accusation in his statement. The 'seminars' were voluntary: I conceived of them as a kind of group therapy, absolutely not my cup of tea. His shoes were actually a lighter grey than his light suit, with its double-breasted jacket and faint mauve stripe. The snugly-fitting striped tie was possibly a genuine tie of a school or even regiment. His hair, shining as the starlings, was abundant but neatly cut. One could not whole-heartedly approve of his turn-out, but it was undoubtedly effective.

'There's so much to do at Stares, and that has to be done, I've never found the time, I'm afraid.'

'But I hear you've set up a rival activity, Mr Toyne, which I'm not sure isn't taking away some of my customers.' He turned an amused look on Mrs Stogden and Mr Chiswell. His English was accented, but the syntax was unerring.

'We have a tiny cast compared with yours, Doctor,' I said.

'You know, involvement in the drama, in imaginary troubles, isn't half a bad idea. But soon you'll be leaving us, Mr Toyne, and there would be no one to carry such a thing on. That is the sadness of Stares. The sadness and the challenge. It is like the life of a school or university, speeded up as in some film about the growth of flora. Just as we are getting to know our intake – whoosh, and they're off.'

'But don't you get some of them back?' said Mrs Stogden.

'Remarkably few, my dear. At the moment not a single one. We shall probably never see you three again. It is at once our regret and triumph.' Dr Singh got up and left us, no hesitancy in his action. It was an effective little performance, if you admired that sort of thing, probably (like the persona of Dr Stembridge) appealing more to women than men.

Mr Chiswell rose in his turn. 'I must be off at once to massage,' he said. 'I dared hardly go while Dr Singh was here, in case he thought that that, too, was infringing on his seminars.'

'Have you taken up massage?' Heather Stogden enquired when Mr Chiswell had left us.

'I have, as a matter of fact.' There was no doubt that when Dr Stembridge had mentioned the facility, my imagination had taken a lubricious turn. But massage proved to be in the hands of a stout lady, asked to be addressed not as Mrs Bamforth but 'Molly'. 'The theory is it reduces blood pressure, relaxes, and results in an extra hour or two of sleep, to say nothing of its effect on digestion and nerves generally.'

'It seemed to me to be on the road to yogi and acupuncture and so forth,' Mrs Stogden said.

'Hard to say nowadays where medicine stops and quackery takes over. It really boils down to "the patient must minister to himself".'

'I thought it was unlucky for an actor to quote from the Scottish play.'

I laughed. 'I'm not sure much more ill-luck can befall me.'

'Well,' said Mrs Stogden, 'at least you're not likely to undergo what Hilary Chiswell had been telling me about. A stray bullet at the Istanbul Airport killed his grandson.'

'Oh Lord.'

'He says why didn't he think to enfold the boy in his arms just as soon as the shooting started.'

'He's blaming himself?'

'Yes, and it was his idea to take the boy on the trip. A weekend break in Istanbul. In retrospect the thing seems crazy, so he says.'

I could see that the blame was worse than my blame. 'But could he have protected the boy effectively?'

'Who knows? At least he himself wouldn't have survived unscathed.'

That was the trouble: surviving in the same physical envelope, but haunted by guilt. 'He told me he was in the Istanbul affair, but nothing of this.'

'It was harrowing hearing it almost casually in the drawing-room just before lunch.'

'Perhaps what you said to him as Polena in the play prompted him to confide. Asking him to take you away from your husband even at that late stage in your relations, even at the end of life renouncing secrecy and falsehood.'

'It might be so,' she said. 'It's upset me.'

'You both seemed composed just now when I joined you.'

'I think he was glad to have spoken of it. I don't know. What can be done for him?'

I thought about Lorna Cochrane, too. By the side of Mr Chiswell's, her troubles were almost farcical. It was perhaps inevitable that at Stares one should eventually hear confessions, but then in ordinary society also there were universal secrets, though the lives that contained them were usually not neurotic enough to let them out.

Then Heather Stogden made an observation that at the time, in the context of confessions, seemed not awfully *outré*: later I pondered it, wondered about it.

'Have you ever thought the familiar faces we see are simply masks that can be removed to reveal underneath something quite appalling? Will be taken off, in fact . . . some day.'

I muttered a sort of denial which at the same time did not exclude the possibility of myself, too, being eventually convinced of the essential vileness of the human.

18

ONCE, except on the matinée day, I almost always used to take a siesta, actually getting into bed, and, whether I'd had a drinking lunch or not, dropping off at once. These days, though sometimes as I read, my hands becoming relaxed through invading sleep, the book slipped through them, as soon as I put the book aside and settled down, a pulse started to throb in my temple, and I was wide awake, remote from sleep, nerves jangled. I believe this and other reversals of good habits and marks of physical well-being, dated from the months of Sammy's severest conduct towards me, possibly even to be pin-pointed to the strange night of interrupted sleep I spent in Canterbury.

Leaving Heather Stogden on the terrace I'd come to my bedroom. Through the open door of the Red Drawing-room I'd seen Mrs Cochrane and Mrs Doggett sitting over their coffee cups, but funked going to them. Still lying on the bed after my foiled siesta, I'd felt too weary to take up my book again, and my thoughts reconstructing the past turned, as they so often did, to Sammy. If I'd been set to write the later dialogues of our quarrels I should have utterly failed, for I couldn't now see how he could constantly have put me in the wrong when I was always amenable, rational, longing for harmony, when I had stopped trying to defend myself, stopped categorically denying accusations of guilt. Yet again, like watching a conjuror, I tried to analyse the trick – the word had to be used – of imputing to me feelings or habits he had himself invented to justify – and cause – his rancour. The utterly familiar formula was: 'You never this – you always the other'. As the amount of drink taken on board increased, so did the vehemence of his accusations – shouted, if necessary, from other rooms or even from house to garden. The defence of my behaviour – even the ignoring of his – was exhausting, like a boxer on his guard against a constantly demonic opponent, and although it was a relief when at last he went off to bed to sleep the booze off, I was usually unfit for any task that had kept me in the house during his tirades. I might simply prepare some supper for myself and eat it in front of the television set. It grew to be the case that Sammy missed supper, missed programmes and old films that in normal days he would have loved. The absence of such shared trivial domesticities undoubtedly helped to slacken the bond between us. It was ironical that at this epoch he had virtually stopped trying to hurt me by silently leaving the house, boasting in due course of encounters, conquests. Drinking and quarrelling, playing and sleeping, occupied the bulk of his time. And in fact he showed (or feigned) a morbid jealousy of me, any social expedition or contact on my part translated in his mind to erotic significance. In that area, also, his accusations were unfounded.

For, as to love, that seemed to have left my life the evening when Sammy made it plain that love for me had left his. Again, I would find it impossible to recover what was said, how far our antagonism had got, on that crucial occasion. Indeed, perhaps only in retrospect did the evening seem crucial at all. Suddenly, as I remonstrated with him about something quite commonplace, my voice thickened and broke. I left him before the tears came down and afterwards was uncertain whether he had observed my emotion or not. I locked the door of my room and wept – possibly indulgently at first, but then with true grief, almost inexhaustibly, unparalleled since child-hood, and then really only in a kind of play-acting – as once, unjustly exiled to my bedroom, I had nibbled at a biscuit through my tears, envisaging it saving me from starvation if I rationed it over the days of incarceration. All the foundations of my relationship with Sammy had vanished – that was the source of my pain – the assumptions of years discovered to be erroneous, nugatory. The weeping over, I was left with a commonplace headache. When eventually we encountered each other again I had the ghost of an expectation of finding his love revived, but of course we were in fact further down the road of mutual isolation.

Did I even at that time speculate if it was some flaw in me that had cancelled his love? Certainly the thought had often recently occurred, and a heartburn of remorse arisen at growing over the years the less able to express physically my affection, my reliance on his very presence – even to put such things in words. But at first surely it seemed a mystery of growing into middle-age that Sammy, once so lively and loquacious, the object not only of my love but my admiration, had become quarrelsome, drunken, often impossible. How could it have been foretold that Sammy would turn out to resemble my father rather than my ideal? All the same, a remark of his when we were still close had always stuck in my mind: 'without lines written for them by others, actors are bores'. It was made during a very convivial dinner party, but I wondered at his being so wounding, however unconsciously.

With sudden resolution I swung my legs off the bed,

and sat up, trying to disperse the stupor of post-lunch and remorse about the past. It was the hour of Dr Singh's 'seminars'. Perhaps I ought to attend them. It seemed foolish to be paying so much and yet have blank periods in the day. I slipped into my shoes and combed my hair. When I opened the bedroom door it gave me a shock to find Paul Vickerman standing there. 'Hello. Were you coming to see me?' It was all I could think of to say. On his part, he said nothing. The next moment I saw what was more than usually odd about him. 'My goodness, you've shaved your whiskers off.' He didn't respond to this, either. 'I was just going to walk out. Shall we go together?'

Obediently, like a child, he accompanied me at my side down the corridor, and at last said: 'I can't go on with the play-reading.'

'Oh, I'm sorry to hear that. You were doing so well.'

'I was interested in the artistic connotations. But he tries to shoot himself.'

'Yes, that's true.' Astonishingly enough, I'd never considered the bearing on Paul of Constantin's actions in the play. Paul didn't say, possibly hadn't yet got that far, that in the end Constantin succeeds in committing suicide.

'I couldn't do that,' Paul said.

We began to descend one of the two staircases that led to the hall. All was deserted at this hour of the afternoon. As ever, I found it difficult to keep converse with Paul on some common level of reality. 'Well, if you feel the play is . . . hurting your recovery here you must certainly opt out. But we'll all be very sorry to lose you from our ranks.'

'You see,' he said, 'the other shooting doesn't help. He's actually been killed.'

'You mean . . .?'

'The President's been killed. Haven't you read about it, even viewed it on TV?'

In a way, Paul was at his most coherent, yet the process of his thought and feelings seemed quite abstruse.

'Yes. Awful.'

'It may be the first step in the final consequence.'

I thought of Constantin's 'play within a play'–'All is cold, cold, cold!' Yes, everyone saw what might be the outcome of the Middle East kerfuffle, the nuclear powers drawn in, some militarily logical first step, but were we as serious as Paul about it? It could be said that his derangement was by no means an exaggerated reaction to the state of the nations.

'We've been through worse crises since the war.'

He made no reply to this inadequate remark, but stayed at my side as we left the hall, out towards what seemed to be the eternal sunlight. It occurred to me that I still might persuade the new boy, David Waddilove, to take part in the play, in which case he could read Constantin. I said to Paul: 'We don't want to lose you altogether. Will you do the little role of Yakov, and also read the stage directions? That's a job still going.'

He did not reply to this, but said: 'I have my own means of keeping abreast with world news, as you probably realize.'

In my turn, I did not reply to that, too cowardly to probe the extent of his illusions. I was rather glad when we came across Mary Gow sitting on the stone steps that led from the terrace to the garden. She was wearing blue jeans, and I saw for the first time how long and lean her legs were. Her elbows rested on her knees, hands holding her head, brown hair falling forward. Though she must have heard our footsteps, she was in no hurry to raise her head and look at us. I stopped beside her and said: 'Hello.' Paul went down a few more steps. Seeing them together, it struck me in a fatheaded sort of way that I might ameliorate the roles they had been playing in the Chekhov. I said to her: 'What lesson are you playing truant from?' Even to myself I sounded middle-aged, not to say ancient.

'Don't know,' she said – a schoolgirl's answer.

A whiff of newly-mown grass came up the steps. 'I think they've cut the lawn at last. What about a vigorous game of clock-golf to give us an appetite for tea?' The asinine facetiousness was entirely due to the company of these youngsters. Had I somewhere along the years with Sammy quite lost my fellowship with youth?

Almost to my surprise she said: 'All right,' and rose to her feet. One step above me, she towered over me, bringing back the countless occasions when I'd been dwarfed by a female character, especially since in recent years affluence and sensible diet had bred a race of giantesses.

'What's your record for the course?' I asked her, as we all set off for the level stretch of lawn before it descended to the wall that separated garden from park.

'I've never played here before.'

Her putting was probably going to be like her bridge. If one of the objects of Stares was to enure its clients to a tame life, this was an apt occasion. The implements of the game were kept in a storehouse beneath the terrace, access from the lawn itself. I went in to find three putters and three golf-balls among the garden furniture. It was the spider season: I felt my face and hair breaking the gossamer in the storehouse gloom. When I emerged, Mary was alone.

'What happened to Paul?'

'He vamoosed.'

'Without a word?'

'Without a single word.'

'I'm not really surprised.'

'No, I couldn't imagine him playing clock-golf.'

'But you can imagine me?' I asked.

She reached out to take one of the clubs. 'Come on. I'll beat you. My father used to make me play golf.'

As we moved over to numeral 1, I said: 'Paul's not going on with the play. I thought I'd try to get this new young man, David Waddilove, to take his place. Have you met him? Do you fancy him as a hopeless suitor?'

'Don't care.'

She won the toss and bent over her shot with quite a professional crouch, her hair once again descending, in a tangled fashion. With the mowing and the dry weather, the course was very fast, but when she got the pace of it she was pretty expert. Each 'hole' was ostensibly much the same, but there were declivities in the lawn and a general slope to it that differentiated them in fact. However, my previous experience of the course availed little. After two or three holes she said: 'What did we agree? Fifty pence a hole?'

'Not likely. This is for love.'

'Ah.'

What experience did the monosyllable imply? There was no doubt that on her own Mary Gow was a different article from the reluctant bridge fourth or the girl suffering a visit from her parents. At five o'clock she said: 'Paul told me he was chucking the play-reading. I ought to warn you that I, too, am not a certainty.'

'Oh, come on. You're not going to rat on me. Your reading is very good, gets better all the time.'

'I've dropped out of everything I've ever gone in for. Every school I ever went to . . .' As if to contradict herself, she stroked her ball to within a foot of this tricky hole.

'The point is at Stares not to drop out of anything.

—131—

That's why so much is voluntary – too much, some would say.'

'I didn't necessarily accept the Stares philosophy by coming here – any more than I accepted a school's by turning up at the start of the term.'

'Persevere as a favour to me.'

She gave me one of her rare direct looks. 'Why are you in here? You're successful, quite famous. Shouldn't think you've ever dropped out.'

' "*In* here". You make it sound like a jail.'

'I expect our friends and relatives wish it was. But really, why are you here?'

'Bereavement,' I said, automatically using Fred Boraston's term. 'That led to my finding it impossible to go on being successful, as you call it.'

'And are you being done good to?'

'Too soon to say.'

'Is the play-reading a help?'

'I'm sure it will be if the cast don't all forsake me.'

She tapped in for a two. I went on: 'Now tell me why you're here.'

Before replying she picked her ball out of the hole and dropped it at six o'clock: 'I had an abortion. In messy circumstances. Had to drop out of pregnancy, too, you see.'

I felt my cheeks go red – through guilt, embarrassment – as I remembered that Act IV of *The Seagull* discloses that Nina had a child, that died. My instinct was to keep quiet, till after a few seconds I realized the futility of that. 'I expect you've read on in the play, and discovered what has happened in the interim between Acts III and IV.'

'I know what you mean. But I didn't connect it with me, with my situation.'

'Paul told me he wasn't going on because of Constantin's suicide attempt – and eventual success, I

—132—

suppose. It would contradict his own character.'

'Do you think that's a bluff? He may actually have tried.'

'It's true his words were that he couldn't shoot himself, not kill himself.' I thought how bizarre it was to be discussing death with a young girl in the middle of a not altogether unidiotic pastime.

She removed a few brown crumbs of leaves likely to impede her second shot. 'I expect a lot of people here have thought seriously of killing themselves, if not actually getting down to it.'

Again she scored a two. She added: 'Paul's shaved his beard off, did you notice? While he had the razor at his throat he may well have been tempted to dig deeper with it.' She could surely have had no idea why at those words I once more felt myself violently reddening.

Her tone had been casual, uncaring, the comparative amenability and frankness shown during the game not necessarily a permanent feature of her present state. Her turning up at the evening's read-through of Act III seemed much in doubt. And as if to emphasize this, while I was putting the things back in the storehouse at the end of our game, she disappeared as suddenly as had Paul.

Going up the steps to the terrace I fell in with Fred Boraston, and we brought our tea and biscuits out to one of the terrace tables.

'Did you ever probe Maida about her past?' I asked him when we'd settled down.

He averted his pale face. 'Never had the chance. In any case, I'm afraid I let my imagination get the better of me over snooker the other day.'

'I'm finding her more and more forthcoming. Perhaps not as daunting as you thought.'

He bit into a biscuit with his elaborate bridge-work.

I went on: 'As to imagination, don't you think it better to let it emerge into the light of day, to share it to some degree?'

'Well,' he said, 'I find I quite relish this play-reading of yours.'

'I'm glad.'

'For one thing, it takes me back to my early days when I did a lot of court work, and was keen to succeed in it, studying ways to improve my performances. Rather like a young actor, I imagine. And I was newly married – to my first wife. Happy days, though at the time there were great worries – threat of war, my wife pregnant with Maida – my daughter, I mean – quite penurious on my salary as an assistant solicitor, a mere dogsbody. I suppose I was never as happy again, and certainly never will be.'

'Who knows if you won't in the end sail into an extraordinary mildness, as the poet said?'

'Mildness? Yes, I suppose most of us want that quality in our lives.'

'All except the maniacs of the Middle East.'

'Yes, yes. It was the same when I was young, but then the maniacs were Italians and Germans and Japs.'

'Though you could argue,' I said, 'that in every society there were the cruel and the kind, the violent and the peaceful, the bold and the timid.'

'Come to that,' he said, 'such contrasts lurk in every human breast.'

'At Stares, undoubtedly timidity has the upper hand.'

Mr Boraston laughed. 'Yes, we're all pretty well cowed. It's strange, too, how on coming here we hide our symptoms. Sweating, sleeplessness, headaches, even depression – we tend not to betray them. I suppose it's a consequence of finding others in the same boat.'

Suddenly his face became immensely serious, and he blurted out, in a manner utterly unlike anything shown before: 'I've never told anyone, not even Stembridge, of an awful dream that's only just stopped recurring during the last few days . . . a stone urn, hanging from a number of chains, elaborately looped, in empty space . . . no meaning whatever.'

Somehow, his sparse words conveyed the nightmarish sense evidently experienced.

'I can see,' I began.

But he saved me a comment by saying quickly: 'I dread them starting again. The urn turns and recedes, yet stays in view. Something cosmic, frightening.'

'Isn't it a good sign that the dream is less frequent?'

I saw his features break once again into a smile, as he took up his teacup, and exchanged a word or two with Miss Stittle, she coming from behind me and hobbling slowly past. Had even she bad dreams?

19

THE cast were to assemble in the White Drawing-room after dinner. Surprisingly enough, both Paul and David Waddilove appeared. I said to Paul, 'I thought you'd quit.'

'You said I was doing well and I've decided that's what I want to do.'

'Are you going to carry on with Constantin or take on Yakov and the stage directions?'

'Carry on.'

It seemed that Stares, or even the play-reading, was having some effect. Minus his sketchy whiskers and in the slightly more formal garb he had put on for dinner, he looked much less odd. To David Waddilove I said: 'I'm glad you've come.'

'At dinner I sat at the same table as Mary – I don't know her other name – and she persuaded me, but now she doesn't seem to be here.'

'You'll have to share a copy, so see you sit next to someone who has one. Act III is where Yakov has his big chance – two speeches, all of three lines.'

Mary Gow came in late. I said: 'I thought the clock-golf had exhausted you, and you weren't going to turn up.'

'I got someone to play the servant for you, so don't grumble.'

'Full marks.' My reply hid a surprise at Mary Gow's near sprightliness of tone, greatly different from her previous behaviour, for instance at the bridge-table.

She would not have been so 'cheeky' to her parents, I felt sure. It might be that her various 'droppings-out' had an element in them of rebellion as well as of mere sullenness.

The reading started at last and we soon came to what I'd thought of as the incendiary words in this Act, Masha saying, after she's persuaded Trigorin to have another drink: 'Women drink more often than you think. The minority drink openly, like me; the majority do it on the sly. And it's always vodka or brandy.' But most usually gin, one couldn't help thinking in the context of Stares. Possibly all the four ladies of the cast – Mrs Cochrane, Maida Brown, Heather Stogden, Mary Gow – had raised the elbow at some stage of their diverse troubles, maybe even now in thrall to the demon drink. One often thought of the subject in semi-facetious terms – bottles in unlikely concealment, the piling up of empties, the music-hall element in drunkenness – but the addiction was especially devastating in the realm of human affection, so what could be worse? Sammy drunk was an impossible person, and Sammy sober, between drunken hours, was an utterly different character from his pre-drunken days – shallower, of shrivelled emotions, indolent, carping. I used to wonder whether alcohol had released or implanted the malice in his drunken persona: one could see that in his sober intervals the faults were mere exaggerations of those all have to battle against.

It's in the same speech that Masha says to Trigorin: 'You're a simple soul. I'm sorry to see you go.' It is typical of Chekhov's acuteness that he so describes the all-seeing intellectual of the play – indeed, Trigorin is the character who through his asides and notebook entries really reveals the springs of his conduct the most. The rest, for all their catch-phrases and *idées fixes*, could be said to be the more complicated, certainly mysterious. It was the simple soul aspect of Trigorin that fitted the reality of my own, though whether any denizen of Stares – even Maida, who had to utter the line – would have seen it I suppose might be doubted. What would they do in the future, these Chekhovian cartoons, to further their loves, their obsessions, their fears? Quite impossible to say.

This Act, too, contains Constantin's telling criticism of Trigorin's talent and character. It comes while Madame Arkadin is changing the dressing on Constantin's head wound, sustained in his suicide attempt. He says that he and his mother are virtually quarrelling on Trigorin's account, yet elsewhere Trigorin is laughing at everyone, trying to educate Nina, convince her of his genius. Madame Arkadin argues in vain that Constantin is simply envious, that to people without talent, merely with pretensions, the only thing left is to abuse real talent. How often had I thought, as I moved towards middle-age, particularly after I'd started to write, that art – both acting and imaginative prose – had moved on (or elsewhere), leaving me outmoded, however sustained by engagements and publication. Sammy, too, had come to seem fixed in a musical style of a certain epoch; his triumphs in the byways of the art, like film music. It might have been that seeing this himself, keeping quiet about it, had contributed to the devasting changes in him. No doubt one comes to settle for eventual disappointment as to the extent of one's talent, but to give up the notion that when all is said and done one possesses true originality, and spawns lasting achievement, is crushingly self-destructive. I was still far from that, though what would have happened had I stayed in my agitated environment instead of moving into the relief of Stares, *quien sabe*? as D H Lawrence, that early hero of mine, had the pretentious habit of writing.

By similar tokens, wouldn't I now, if a suitable young man were about, try to impress him with my artistic experience, even encourage his intellectuality, while at the same time pursuing his physicality? To find a seagull beside the lake! As it was, I apostrophized Mary Gow across the other seated readers – those wonderful eyes, inexpressibly beautiful smile, those gentle features of angelic purity – and our 'prolonged kiss' was a mere stage direction inserted by the newcomer to our troupe. I wondered if the words of the play had any effect on her. Just before the curtain falls on Nina and Trigorin's kiss, she has announced her determination to go on the stage: 'Tomorrow I shan't be here. I'm leaving my father, everything. I'm starting a new life . . .' By this time she was one of the readers who had best learnt the lesson I'd tried to instil – don't hurry – and the speech was so effective that escaping in real life from the thralldom of her family seemed quite on the cards, if her entry into my profession a little less so.

After the reading I sought out Lorna Cochrane and drew her aside from the chattering group she was in. 'Your sister wasn't with you at dinner.'

'She's going home first thing in the morning. Still *my* home, I'm afraid.'

'But that must be a relief.'

'Of course, I paid her off. Yes, I paid her off. I was too frightened to hang on, in case she blabbed.'

'I think you were wise.'

'I've still got to face her when I leave here. That's what haunts me.'

'I wish I could help.' It was a facile remark, since the chances of my becoming involved in her future life must be nil – though a vision of giving a poetry-reading in Crewe came wildly to mind.

'You have helped,' said Mrs Cochrane. As Paul Vickerman passed us she caught hold of his sleeve. 'I hope we're still friends after our quarrel,' she said to him with a laugh that was not altogether lighthearted. 'We say such awful things to each other in that play.'

'I think Paul's going to see the character through to the bitter end, and it is bitter in the last Act.' I didn't quite know what to say, and a hiatus loomed ahead in the conversation, for Paul simply stood looking into the middle-distance with a slight smile. The removal of his whiskers had revealed two vertical lines near the corners of his mouth, not deep but now a feature of his face, rather attractive. Of all the people I'd come to know at Stares he was certainly the most disconcerting.

Rather on the lines of my own thoughts, Mrs Cochrane said: 'I suppose in the theatre people are used to keeping their real lives and their dramatic lives quite separate.'

'I think one's fellow players in any play evolve entirely fresh characters – a blend of the person one already knows, and that person's bringing the part to life.'

Paul's silence and smile persisted – a pitying smile, it might be called. I suddenly felt like kicking him up the backside, perhaps a common reaction to the deranged. But as we moved away to the hall and the pre-prandial bar, he said to me quietly: 'I know that Mrs Cochrane may have been substituted.' Before I could think of any response to this, he walked off into the little procession of the rest of the cast.

I made a point of again thanking David Waddilove for coming to the reading, and reassuring him about his performance. He was sitting alone in the Red Drawing-room, a copy of one of the glossy periodicals available open on his knees. Could he be interested in buying canterburys and commodes?

'To tell you the truth,' he replied, 'it wasn't only Mary who encouraged me to come. Dr Pentecost mentioned it, said I ought to involve myself if I could.'

Dr Pentecost was a youngish man who drove a red MG, at the moment taking advantage of the phenomenal weather by having the soft top habitually down. I guessed he was not on the staff but merely a visiting physician or psychiatrist, maybe engaged to fill in during Dr Mowle's absence.

'I'd no idea Dr Pentecost knew about *The Seagull*, let alone approved of it as an adjunct to his therapy. But then judging by his motor-car he's probably willing to take a chance.'

A deep blush came to David Waddilove's pale countenance. What *faux pas* had I committed? I blundered on about Stembridge seeming less enthusiastic, but my words washed over David, who said eventually: 'It was an MG I was driving. I daresay you didn't know.'

'No.' I pondered for a moment. 'I'm afraid I don't know anything at all.'

'I killed my girl-friend in a car crash.' After the blush, the previously somewhat strangled phrases, these words came out as though he had rehearsed them or said them often. And it seemed to me that at Stares I had become practised in responding to revelations embarrassing or harrowing, reacting acceptably where once I would have found it scarcely possible to be other than tongue tied. It wasn't that my feelings had become hardened or facile, but that I'd found a social mode for their expression.

'Oh, my dear, how terrible.'

'Yes.' He closed his magazine with a trembling hand. 'I tend to think everyone here knows about . . . my plight. That's why . . .'

'You probably realize that most people are here because of some precipitating trauma. I believe there's consolation in that.'

'I've not been here long enough to know what others

. . . It's only recently I've been able to speak about what happened.'

'We're all in a sort of drama really. Awful events have happened, coincidences fallen; everything's more condensed and sensational than in ordinary life.'

'As you can see,' he said, 'I came out of it without a scratch. The other driver, too, more or less. Elizabeth was killed outright, as everyone calls it.'

I dared hardly say anything more, feeling I'd been sententious enough. But soon he went on: 'It wasn't my fault. The other driver's being prosecuted. But that's neither here nor there, strange to say.'

'I can see that.'

'I called her my girl-friend because so many speak like that these days, but we intended to marry.' He transferred the magazine from his knees to the low table in front of us. 'My parents thought I ought to come here. You see, I knew Elizabeth was dead, but I didn't feel she was dead. My belief in what had happened was – was – suspended. Can you imagine that? Perhaps that was so because of my guilt. If I hadn't taken her out – along that road . . .'

While these all too serious words were being spoken, I'd seen out of the corner of my eye Walter, who must have already come on night duty at reception, serving drinks to a nearby couple. He now came up to us. 'I'll just move this book,' he said, referring to the magazine, 'off the little table, then there'll be room for your drinks in due course. It'll be with the other books on the table in the corner if you should want to look at it again. Perhaps you'd like to have your drinks now, while you're enjoying your chat.' Once again I felt beneath his words and manner the implication that he had, so to speak, rumbled me, knew my erotic tastes out of a breadth of experience by no means confined to expensive establishments like Stares – perhaps in the

Forces or the Merchant Navy – and that he compre-
hended without exactly pardoning.

'Will you have something?' I asked David.

He shook his head.

'Well,' said Walter, 'if you change your mind I shall
be at the desk, or you can touch the bell over there. In
any case, I fully expect to be coming in and out of this
room for quite some time yet.'

When Walter had gone, I sat silent, feeling it
impossible to comment on Walter, say, to call attention to his Chekhovian characteristics – the sort of
repetitiveness Chekhov might have used had he
decided to develop the very character David was
reading in *The Seagull*; impossible to descend from the
intensity of the young man's previous words. At length
he said: 'I still don't feel she's dead.'

The words did not make the situation any easier. It
was the suspension of belief rather than of disbelief, I
thought, that was needed tolerably to see the drama
through.

That night I dreamt of my grandmother (my
mother's mother), my saying to her: 'I think you're
going to make it to a hundred.' In the dream my
mother was dead, as she was in reality. My grandmother had in fact died in my boyhood. I woke immediately following the dream, and turned these matters
over in my mind. What was there for Dr Stembridge?
Nothing really – for little signified in my having
been in a way closer (like the Narrator in Proust)
to my grandmother than my mother. That could be
explained by my grandmother not having had to
endure the rebellions and follies of my adolescence.
Vaguer images surrounded the dream, almost irre-
coverable, fading fast, essentially fantastic: these,
could they be fixed and explained, might help to solve
the riddles of one's personality and existence.

20

' "OUR lives are passing away," ' said Heather Stogden, quoting from Polena Andreyevna, her character in the play.

' "We can't do anything about that," ' I replied, in the words of Madame Arkadin. Looking at Mrs Stogden in the mid-morning light coming off the lake, I thought how apt were her words: the remnants of her beauty were undoubtedly there, but very much under attack. No doubt she slept as badly as any of us, being weaned by Stembridge from her syrops. The elaborate structure of her hair seemed more precarious than ever, the skin round her eyes sallower, more vulnerable.

'But in a sense,' she said, 'life here seems suspended.'

I thought of David Waddilove's confession the previous night. 'Part of that feeling may be due to the weather,' I said.

'Yes, it really is phenomenal. Though I heard on my transistor that a change is on its way.'

'Another thing is that one's volition has been committed to others.'

'Well,' she said, 'that may be so, but I for one keep thinking about what's going to happen when I leave.'

'There ought to be something like the Prisoners' Aid Society.' But the reflex facetiousness covered a pang of anxiety. Was I going to return to the old desolation?

We had been to Noel Mummery's art session: clay modelling – activity even nearer than gouache to the

—144—

coprophilous implications of art, resented by the instructor. All had worn the green smocks available: now Mrs Stogden's garb was revealed. I broke the silence following my last remark by saying: 'I like your suit.' It was knitted, subdued purple, well-cut.

'Do you?' She brightened considerably. 'Yes, it is nice. It came from Simpsons. One of Stogden's rare acts of generosity, prompted by guilt. He wanted the best of both worlds – his fun and my income. D'you know, the bastard counter-petitioned, alleging adultery? Simply dreamed up by him to try to get out of paying maintenance.'

'Tch.'

'But divorcées are the last people who ought to talk about divorce,' she said.

We had got within sight of the boathouse, which Mrs Cochrane had rounded on the morning of her confession. Actually from within there now appeared a different female figure, soon identifiable as Denise, already dressed for her role in the dining-room. She cut across the grass instead of keeping to the path, and so avoided us. There was not much of an interval before Noel Mummery also emerged, but he at once turned away, and soon disappeared in the distance under the trees.

'Where can he be going if not to evade us?' Mrs Stogden enquired.

'You can probably get out of the park that way, and into the village. He has a house there.'

'Is he married then?'

'Yes, complete with children and resident mother-in-law. And a wife not too well.'

'Are you implying a reasonable excuse for matrimonial deceit?'

'Absolutely not.'

'What about Denise?'

'I know nothing of her. I don't know much about Noel, really. He once invited me into his house for a beer, but his family were not to be seen.'

'He's obviously one of those genial villains,' she pronounced.

'Aren't you reading rather a lot into what may have been an accidental, even an innocent, encounter?'

'No.'

I thought of Noel embarking on a mess-up of his married life, perhaps leading the pair to a place like Stares. Or it might have been Mrs Mummery who had set the slow explosive device. I said something of this, adding: 'One imagines amatory enterprise also to be in a state of suspension at Stares, don't you think?'

'Well, maybe among the paying public,' said Mrs Stogden. 'But Mummery and Denise are supposed to be normal.' She laughed. 'You'd expect the warders to set an example to the inmates.'

'They did use the cover of the boathouse.'

'We'd better turn back in case anyone else emerges,' said Mrs Stogden.

'Do you think they saw us?'

'Denise certainly. It looked as though the Arts Director intended to right-turn anyway.'

'It may be embarrassing being shown to one's place at lunch.'

'As far as I'm concerned, the embarrassment will be all on her side,' said Mrs Stogden.

'Women are much tougher than men in such matters,' I said. 'But Noel Mummery's transferring to the patients is not quite so likely as the chamber-maid who does my room.'

'Oh, you mean Maud.'

'Is that what she's called? Pallid, black fringe, smile with a missing tooth.'

'Yes. And yawns a lot.'

'This morning she said: "I expect you wonder why I'm smiling. Everybody wonders. But I shall never, never tell." Those were the first words she'd ever addressed to me.'

'She wouldn't be bad-looking with a touch of make-up and a bit of bridge-work.'

'Bonny Maud, merry mad Maud.'

'Is that a quotation?' enquired Mrs Stogden.

' "Tom o' Bedlam's Song".'

'I say!'

By the time we reached the garden a number of people were converging for pre-lunch juices. When I took our potions out on the terrace Heather was talking to Dr Singh, who once again was making his rounds, like some hospital consultant. The Indian summer has brought out the Indian doctor, I thought I would say to Heather when he'd passed on his way. His suit today was even lighter in weight and more bizarre in its stripes; possibly emanating from the lands of his origins. After he had greeted me, he said: 'I see you have a cold sore. But no cold apparently.'

'No. I sometimes get them without any other symptoms of a cold.' His acute eye had to be acknowledged: I had imagined my moustache hid the unsightliness.

'Yes, the virus often unaccountably flares up in those who possess it. You know the sore is caused by a virus, of course.'

'I think I do.' I was not keen on my body being discussed in public, even as a purely scientific phenomenon.

'It is a herpes infection. The virus is closely related to that of venereal disease, to be brutally frank.' Dr Singh laughed his rather hissing laugh. 'It is thought that the two strains separated aeons ago when certain primates adopted an erect posture, and face to face sexual congress. Isn't that interesting? So all we have to do is simply to look round for the visible evidence on the lips of other patients here.'

'You will look in vain,' I said. I couldn't help being amused.

'It so happens, Doctor,' said Mrs Stogden, with a straight face, 'that Mr Toyne and I have just been having a discussion on similar lines.'

For a moment Dr Singh seemed nonplussed, perhaps upset that he might have to move on without having the last clinching word. Then he said: 'I should have added that the spread of the virus was greatly assisted by your sex becoming continuously instead of only intermittently attractive, Mrs Stogden.'

It was a good exit line. When he had gone, Heather said: 'I wonder whether the amatory really can be suspended, anywhere.'

'Monasteries and nunneries?'

'The amatory's there in its most concentrated form, I expect.'

21

BY juggling one or two appointments, we managed to arrange the Act IV read-through for the late afternoon following Dr Singh's little herpes lecture. As the cast assembled in the White Drawing-room I thought how my view of each of them had changed during the process of the read-through, not least of Noel Mummery that very day. On the portrait of the simple, stout, domesticated, hail-fellow-well-met painter, had to be superimposed the lineaments found attractive by a rather attractive girl. Though something more lively in her had briefly manifested itself, Mary Gow seemed to have sunk back into her sullen-looking silence. Mr Charley I now thought more supportable than at the time Mr Boraston had taken steps to avoid him by the lake. And so one might go on. How much Chekhov's characterization – in some cases opposing, in others enlarging, real life – had contributed to these amended estimates was difficult to tell. Even more than with professional actors, the characters of *The Seagull* I would henceforth associate with the personae of Stares. As for myself, I wondered if I, too, had suffered modification. The conversations and confessions were perhaps only an intensification of what I had been conscious of for many years – a professional interest in the existences and mannerisms of others, a storing-up of observation that when the time came would enable me convincingly to create a fraudulent chartered accountant, say, or an ambitious politico. Yet at Stares there had been an added dimension: the progress of my own recovery from break-down, if recovery it was; it still had to be tested on stage, as it were. What had the others made of all this? Invisible to them would be my simultaneous identification with and opposition to the Trigorin figure. The development of literary creativeness over the last few years had led me, like any writer, to see mirrored in myself Trigorin's selfishness and exploitation of experience and emotion for the sake of art. But there was an even stronger strand of myself in Constantin – 'failure' as an artist, the contrast with Trigorin's literary 'tricks'. This comes to a head in Act IV in Constantin's excellent speech as he settles down at his desk to write just before finding Nina in the garden: 'I've gone on and on about new forms, but now I feel myself gradually slipping into the old ways. (He reads from his MS.) "The poster on the fence announced . . . a pale face framed by dusky hair . . ." "Announced", "framed"– utterly banal. I'll start with the hero being wakened by the rain, but all the rest has got to go. The description of the moonlight's too long, too laboured. Trigorin would have used the technique he's worked out for himself, made it easy. He'd say "The neck of a broken bottle glittered on the bank, and the shadow of the mill-wheel blackened"– and there's a moonlight night. But I write about the shimmering light, the twinkling stars, a distant piano dying away in the still and scented air. Awful . . . Yes, I'm growing more and more convinced that it isn't a question of old forms or new forms, but what a man writes without thinking of forms, what ideas he pours out from his heart.'

I'd cut nearly all of this for the reading, but there is no doubt that Constantin's realization of his literary failure is intended to be a strong element in his suicide.

If I really felt this in my own case, I could see there would be a catastrophic diminution of my will, my bother, to live. I could better stand the diminution of myself as an actor than as a writer – those two, in a sense opposing, elements of my nature.

How masterly Chekhov's conveying of the lapse of a couple of years between Acts III and IV, not least the reference to the stage in the garden of Act I, now ruined, the curtain flapping in the wind; the school-master's natural mention of his and Masha's baby; and then Sorin in a wheelchair. Even the change in the weather from the previous three Acts seems to mark rather more than a succeeding season. Yes, one assented to the dramatist's argument: at certain epochs in life the elapse of two years, even two months, could change almost the entire pattern of existence.

I wondered whether the women in our cast especially felt the force of some passages in this Act. For instance, Constantin's bare account of Nina's fate in the interim between Acts III and IV: 'She had a child. The child died.' That was an additional factor in the lives of women, at which the mind boggled. And then Polena's remark, so near the banal yet deep at the heart of the play: 'A woman needs nothing, only a kind look. I know that from my own experience.' When Mrs Stogden spoke the words, speculation arose as to how true they were to *her* experience. No doubt there were some, perhaps many, even as attractive physically and mentally as Heather must have been – and indeed was now – who had never earned more than a common-place regard. If a woman's requirements were modest, so too was most men's power to supply them.

Of course, Chekhov in this Act does not neglect the masculine side of lovelessness. Probably few men would come out with Constantin's 'I'm lonely, unwarmed by any affection' – in fact, would scarcely be able so to analyse their lack of happiness – but the condition surely existed more commonly than might be supposed. Strange to say, I would not have readily identified it in myself after Sammy had withdrawn, or ceased to be able to feel, his love, despite the crisis of estrangement. Men sense they are strong, self-sufficient, and, in the last analysis, capable of further conquests. Jealousy is their Achilles heel, and it is significant that in *The Seagull* the one character who is disturbed by that emotion is Constantin.

Another train of thought was prompted by Constantin's sense of this artistic failure – the promising start of Sammy's career, which in the end could be said to have been downhill all the way, in fact was almost as briefly and dismissively characterized by *The Times*'s obituarist. When I first met him, his reputation was already familiar. As a boy at school I knew of the first performance of his first symphony, an occasion of some *éclat*, both because of the composer's youth and his being the son of one of the principals in the work's performers, the Royal Philharmonic Orchestra, a woodwind player who had become a 'name' because of her chamber-music work. The occasion was an artistic success, and the symphony received several subsequent performances, including the Proms. Even Sammy's face became familiar – full yet handsome, eyes pale, hair curling.

We encountered during the productions of The Poetic Theatre – usually one-off Sunday evening occasions. I took small parts, asked to join the company simply because I'd done some verse-reading for the BBC; Sammy was musical director or adviser, composed the incidental and other music, conducted when grants or patrons enabled a small orchestra to be assembled. Even before the first performance in which I appeared I'd seen a programme – MUSIC COMPOSED

AND CONDUCTED BY SAMUEL RANKIN – and been impressed by the authority of the statement. When I thought of Sammy at this stage of this career, very much a part of interesting things going on in various arts, I couldn't help being gnawed by guilt, the sense that I might have done more to keep him on the *qui vive* – even the anxiety that I had actively contributed to his decline; in some Jamesian fictive way feeding my own progress on his. For it was very soon after we met that we set up house together, and so everything we did thereafter became in a way a collaboration.

'I'm a – seagull. No, that's not what I meant to say.'

Nina's repetitive phrase in Act IV had always seemed to me to strike possibly the only false note in the whole play. The words may sound more plausible in Russian, but even so it appears a bit thick to be emphasizing the symbolism so bare-facedly – and really so superfluously. Yet now I saw how an artist at the end of her (or his) tether might so imagine herself, and actually speak such words in a kind of dementia. If some of Sammy's drunken anathemas had been recorded they could well have yielded such, at first blush, implausibilities, rather as Paul Vickerman's *curriculum vitae*, and even his remarks drifted off into dottiness – and he only at the beginnings of the frustrations of creative ambition.

Coming away from the read-through, I accommodated my pace to that of Lorna Cochrane's. 'Well', I said, 'Paul seemed quite imperturbable about his suicide.'

'I'm glad you think so. I've been wondering so much about it.'

'Me, too. But the fictive enactment may not have been a bad thing – though it doesn't do to play the amateur psychoanalyst.'

'I wish I could do something permanently for that

—153—

boy. Rather more than briefly play the part of his mother. He could have my money when I'm dead.' The last phrase came out with vehemence. 'You see, Alice has children as rapacious as she is. They butter me up in their way, but they hope to step in when I'm gone. And before their mother, too, since they know we've never got on. The vultures surround me.'

'What about the traditional cats' home? Or do you feel the obligation is overwhelming after all?'

'I don't know what I feel. Perhaps that's part of the reason I'm here. If I could start again – with Paul, say – in a different place, away from everyone who knows me! But I'm too old, too old. I haven't the will.'

I spoke the words just uttered by the estate manager: ' "We're all growing old and withering away, as the elements beat on us. But you, honoured lady, go on being young – with your light dresses, sprightliness, grace . . ." '

Mrs Cochrane laughed. 'I had mixed feeling about Mr Charley's flattery. I accept yours with gratitude. And that reminds me that I must go and change for dinner.'

'Ah, you're always extremely tony.'

She laughed again. 'Of course, it's years since I heard that word.'

'Did you know it was in *Ulysses* and D H Lawrence?'

'Now you've given me something to live up to.'

When Mrs Cochrane had turned off towards the lift, I caught up with the other old dame with a stick, Miss Stittle. I was half surprised to be greeted by name, and detained by a hand, loosely gloved in wrinkles, on my sleeve. 'Mr Toyne, I'm so looking forward to the play-reading. Is it on Saturday evening, as they say?'

'Yes.' This was my first exchange with her: she seemed far from as gaga as her reputation and appearance suggested. 'God willing.'

—154—

'It will be interesting to watch these people one knows acting out other parts.'

'Yes, I can see that. I hadn't thought about it before.'

'Usually people only have to act their normal parts, so called.' She cackled, no doubt amused at her own insight.

To confirm her point was taken, I said: 'In my profession I'm used to knowing people who act two parts.'

But she had moved on to other thoughts. 'I believe we shall have visitors in the audience, some friends and relations. A pity Mrs Whatshername's sister has gone. Is your wife coming?'

'I'm not married.'

'Oh, what a pity! Are you like me? I would have liked to love and be loved, but it never came my way. No, in all my long life it never came. You must do better. You're still young; you've still plenty of time for romance. Even here, in this . . . funny place, there are opportunities.'

'I suppose so, for some.'

'You ought to shave your beard off. Forgive me for being personal. But you'd shed years, you know. If only I could make such a change in myself!'

Well, I thought, you have at least the makings of a beard. But she may have been referring obliquely to this. There was an ambiguity in many of her remarks, depending on whether one regarded them as studied or spontaneous. She threw off the history of her life in a sentence or two, but what thralldom or tedium they might imply! We had halted in one of two annexes to the main hall, a dimly-lit, panelled no-man's land from which rose one of the two staircases. Again, an attempt had been made to brighten the place with some abstract prints, doubtless taking the place of land-scapes and genre paintings that had also once been fashionable, round about the time Miss Stittle was born. She came closer to me, as though to give me a better sight of her whiskers.

'What's going on here, Mr Toyne? Eh? Where's Dr Mowle? I came here to see him but they don't let me see him.'

'No one apparently sees him at the moment.'

'Once you pay your weekly bill they don't bother. You see any Tom, Dick or Harry. They'll be making me see that dark doctor next. Witch-doctor, I call him.' She laughed again. 'Appropriate for me, I expect you're thinking.'

'Absolutely not.'

'The other young fella shaved his beard off. Great improvement. You take my tip.'

'I grew it for Shakespearean parts, but I may never get any more. So I shall bear your advice in mind.' Taking my cue from Lorna Cochrane, I said: 'I must go and change into something more respectable for dinner.'

As I moved off towards the staircase, I heard her say: 'Have a shave as well. Then you'll look nice for the play.'

22

I was seated next to Maida Brown at dinner. It was not long before she said: 'You seem very interested in our little Denise.'

Certainly my eyes had dwelt on her, thinking of the conjunction with Noel Mummery's round face and spectacles, and heavy body. 'Just an association of ideas.'

'She's attractive.'

'Yes.' As often with Maida, one wondered whether her words signified more than at first appeared.

'Not many attractive girls in this dump. Or men, for that matter.'

'I suppose not.'

'As a matter of fact, I've had a proposal.'

'A proposal?' It crossed my mind that for the first time Maida was revealing some mania, some deviation that had brought her here.

'Not of marriage. A proposal for a rendezvous after we both leave here.'

'Oh. And are you going to reveal the proposer's name. No, let me guess. Not Dr Dorn . . . Sorin.'

She laughed. 'Right first time. But he lives a hundred and fifty miles from me, so it's not likely the meeting will come off.'

'My guess is he has a very substantial solicitor's practice.'

'But it's only a paternal interest. It seems he had a daughter who bore my ghastly name. Perhaps still bears it. He hasn't seen her for donkey's years.'

I wondered whether I ought to open up Fred Boraston's Shakespearean fantasy of finding the person of his lost daughter in Maida. The service of a couple of cutlets each, the placing of a divided dish of sauté potatoes and sprouts, seemed too crude an ambience. Instead, I said: 'The other day it did seem it was Mr Chiswell who interested you.'

'My interest was not exclusive. If these are tender I shall be surprised.' She prodded one of her cutlets. 'Not that I'm obsessed with living in London for ever. Coming here seems to have made a definite hinge in one's life. What happens next could be different. Don't you think?'

'I don't know. It all seems very low key.'

'That may be the secret. Are you under Stembridge or Singh or this new fellow? Can't think of his name. They *are* tough. What's happened to lamb?'

'Wrong time of year.'

'Is that it?'

'I'm under Stembridge,' I said. 'He seems more like a surgeon than a psychiatrist.'

'That's part of his appeal. But I came here to put myself under Dr Mowle. That was the name I was given, as the magician who drove out devils. But where the hell is he?'

'Mr Charley has a theory that he's been found out in some administrative fraud, forced to abdicate.'

'Perhaps he diverted to his own use the money they should have spent on decent food.' She gave up the attack on her cutlets.

As to the improvement of patients at Stares, it seemed to me that during the last three or four days Maida's appearance had changed in a way difficult to define. Was it simply that her lipstick was applied less recklessly, that she had co-ordinated rather than simply thrown on her clothes; or had her manner become more accommodating, she paying some regard to her *vis-à-vis* rather than indulging in a wilfulness that could have been christened childish had it not been accompanied by an intensely feminine scorn or distaste? And as to Fred Boraston's Perdita, I suppose I might casually have asked Maida about Switzerland. But I refrained, as Mr Boraston seemed to have done, reluctant to prick the bubble.

As though confirming my revised estimate of her character, she said out of the blue: 'I think you're marvellous as Trigorin.'

'Thanks.' I expect she had made many blush, not often through words of praise.

'You're careful not to show us up, but all the same . . .'

'Trigorin's the easiest character to play, since he is so self-contained.'

'Is he?' she said. 'I hadn't realized before embarking on this, and listening to you, what technicalities were involved in reading aloud.'

'The technicalities can be overdone. Of course, everyone lacks practice. The Victorians were always reading to each other, and though they may have been hammy, as in their letters and handwriting, I expect they were very effective in their age.'

We had been speaking in quiet tones. My other neighbour was a Lady Hargreaves, almost as ancient-looking as Miss Stittle, possibly at Stares through a mix of bereavement and senility, though the remark she addressed to me by no means suggested any wasting of brain cells. Opposite sat Paul Vickerman, relatively spruce with his tie and shaven face.

'Mr Vickerman has raised an interesting point,' Lady Hargreaves said, 'which my theological ignorance prevents me from answering. If this planet was made for man, why is it going to be extinguished in some cataclysm?'

'Well, I for one don't believe the first part of the proposition.'

'Precisely – that's what I've been saying to Mr Vickerman. There's no problem if the thing is a gigantic accident.'

'Besides, it's not certain we are going to destroy it.'

'Oh,' said Lady Hargreaves, 'he was thinking of a natural cataclysm, like the sun over-heating, or swelling to absorb the planets.'

'That's an event I don't worry about.'

'Very wise. There are enough things in our lifetimes to cause us anxiety.' Like Maida, Lady Hargreaves had abandoned her cutlets, though every now and then she touched her knife and fork with her aged, be-ringed fingers. The third finger of her left hand bore a wedding ring of broad gold and an engagement ring the diamonds and rubies of which were embedded in an equal amount of gold, a romance far in the past of fashion.

Paul was sitting up solemnly, masticating slowly, with an air of dissociation from the proposition conveyed by Lady Hargreaves – or any other except as might concern himself. Why should I worry about him? The thought came with a sense of relief. It was as though his oddity – craziness – was simply a fraud. Playing through Constantin's suicide seemed to have proved his resources to play through life. He might well always be a maniac of a kind, such as one quite amazingly frequently encounters, evading institution-alization if reasonably lucky with relations, friends and cash. I didn't altogether revise this prognosis when, at the end of dinner, we passed out of the dining-room together, and he said: 'Some are planetary risks long before planetary destruction. So I

—160—

shouldn't be too sure of my safety if I were you.'

'Thanks for the warning.'

After dinner, coffee (decaffeinated, acknowledging the endemic insomnia) was available from self-service percolators in both the hall and the Red Drawing-room. At the latter, Mr Chiswell was in front of me, and he half turned and asked if I wanted black or white. We took our cups to a sofa.

'Do you think it right to repeat the *Carmen* song when Dr Dorn returns after discovering Constantin has shot himself?' he asked.

'Absolutely. I'm not sure what effect the Russian original was intended to have – I mean the words about standing spellbound in love are deliberately incongruous, but where the song comes from I've forgotten or never knew. Presumably the piece would be familiar to an average Russian audience. Repeating the *Carmen* melody helps that aspect.'

'Splendid theatrical trick – so simple.' He took a sip of coffee: the cup looked particularly small below his long, benign upper lip. 'After the reading I may go home,' he said, rather self-consciously.

'So soon? You're beating me to it.'

'Worry about my poor old cat is doing me as much harm as the Stares regime is doing me good,' he said, laughing self-disparagingly.

'You are lucky to have altruistic affection to return to.'

'Yes, though I also have to return to associations that will hurt.'

'Heather Stogden told me of your terrible experience in Turkey.' I thought it best to spill the beans.

'Yes. In a way I'm glad to have it known.'

'Some can't tell, and therefore suffer the more.'

'I hope you're within sight of feeling you can leave,' he said.

It crossed my mind that I, too, might 'tell', but how impossible it was I should open up to Mr Chiswell, who despite his benign air still retained an aura of the presumably orthodox moral authority of his head-master's days.

'I haven't thought about it yet.' But even as I spoke these words the future seemed at once to broaden out and change its character, and I realized that it might be possible to lead a life that was not crushed by the effort of surviving day by day, obsessed alternately with drugs and insomnia, depressed by the prospect of any kind of activity.

'You're young,' he said, surely not the first time the words had been spoken to me at Stares. 'I feel myself I haven't life enough left for my sadness to end.'

Yes, I was young, but old enough for the incredible sense of life's inevitable conclusion to strike home. One nevertheless felt almost guilty at having so large an advantage of years.

'And family relations dominate life,' he went on, 'even for grandfathers. Those prospects are saddened as well.'

'I truly sympathize.'

'I value your sympathy. That may help you with your own troubles. I guess many here feel lack of worth.'

Mrs Cochrane and Lady Hargreaves came together into the room, and made laboriously for the coffee percolator.

'I'm glad Mrs Cochrane's sister seems to have vanished from the scene,' observed Hilary Chiswell, in discreet tones. 'Not a good influence.'

'Lorna Cochrane is one who undervalues herself, perhaps after overvaluing herself for most of her life. I doubt she's really shaping up to leave Stares.'

'I wonder. She's quite impressive as Arkadin. If she

could take up her professional work once more . . .'

'Again, that's what many of us ought to do – want to do, in a way. What about Lady Hargreaves?'

'As I understood it, she's just more or less a lonely old widow-woman. A grand dame when Sir Malcolm was alive. Now her occupation's gone. I suppose she might equally be spending a month in a Harrogate hotel. But she may be tussling with drink or drugs, who knows? Most here have a plausible front of manners and appearance.'

'Even Paul Vickerman looks less *outré* than once he did.'

'Stares cures!'

At this moment Fred Boraston came in, looked round, and walked over to us. 'There's a rather good fire visible from the terrace, if you like that sort of thing.'

'Anything for a bit of excitement,' said Mr Chiswell. 'Are you coming?'

We got up and walked out, while Mr Boraston continued to spread the news. I was reminded very much of schooldays, when anything at all out of the routine prompted excitement and hyperactivity. Quite a few had already assembled in the darkness, gazing out over the lake: from them came a buzz of comment. When I'd found a vantage point I saw in the distance a sizeable glow, clouds of sable smoke against the rather darker sky, and, even at my first glimpse, a sudden more extensive glowing and a positive mushroom of smoke, as though from an explosion. I discovered myself next to Mr Charley, who had found the time and resource to arm himself with a pair of binoculars, a voyeuristic auxiliary he might well use for less innocent purposes.

'Where is it?' I asked him.

'Somebody said a fuel dump. Aviation spirit. For those Yankee jets that are always flying over us.'

Noel Mummery materialized on my other side. 'Careless bastards,' he said. 'Someone probably lit up a Camel.' He emitted his violent laugh. It struck me immediately that since he hadn't been at dinner he had come up to Stares to catch Denise when she went off duty. I felt a pang of envy at his forthcoming assignation in the night, the atmosphere crisp but amply mild enough still for amorousness *en plein air*.

From behind I heard Dr Stembridge's voice. 'In my experience Americans are extremely careful – I daresay with matches equally as with anything else.' The Deputy Medical Director had a flat or apartment in Stares, but presumably with no view of the fire. The direction of the voice indicated his enormous advantage over me in height – previously rather more sensed by me than demonstrated by him.

'It might well be the result of a terrorist act,' I said at large. I wondered if Paul was on the terrace. The fire in a way was a confirmation of his view of existence – conspiracy, global communication, cataclysm. Those who thought maniacs were safely segregated in remote areas like the Middle East, brandishing their fists round the coffins of the assassinated, were contradicted.

As though he had read my mind, certainly followed my train of thought, Dr Stembridge said, not without ironic intonation: 'At Stares we're against fires.'

Mr Chiswell was also behind me. 'Doesn't this remind you of another Chekhov work?' he said.

I laughed. 'I know what you mean. Act III of *The Three Sisters*.'

'Chekhov makes it so easy for the fire to be depicted – just the sound of a fire-engine, red flames seen through an open door, talk about the fire. Not much more than our fire tonight.'

'Yes,' I said, 'and of course, unlike our fire – so far as

I know – his fire affects his characters. It's the cause of that wonderful speech by Vershinin when he tells how, when the fire broke out, he rushed home and found his two daughters in their underclothes and his wife not there. And he says to himself: "My God, what things these girls will have to put up with if they live into old age!" Then with the noise, and the street red with fire, and the girls half undressed, he thinks how similar things used to happen many years before, when some enemy invaded, and looted and burned.'

'It all comes back to me,' said Mr Chiswell. 'Wonderful.'

'As so often with Chekhov one wonders if he realized the extent of the irony he put into his situations. Vershinin's comment is that there really is a difference between present and past, implying that in his time there aren't raping and burning invaders. Yet, he says, in two or three hundred years our life will be looked on by people of the future with the same fear and contempt. And in a dozen or so years the German invasions began.'

'To say nothing of even worse medieval horrors in store,' said Mr Chiswell.

'And still going on.'

'You seem to know *The Three Sisters* very well,' said Mr Chiswell.

'I once played Soleni on TV.'

'Do you know, I think I saw that production, but I don't remember you. Is Soleni the . . .?'

'The young officer who kills the Baron in a duel. I played him clean shaven.'

The glow beyond the lake increased in intensity, and seconds later came the sound of an explosion.

' "The exhalations whizzing in the air Give so much light that I may read by them," ' quoted Mr Chiswell.

There was no doubt that without being at all

virulently anti-American, one willed the flames to extend, an attenuated version in oneself of man's ages-long cruelty, a trait I'd imagine absent from Stares, where theoretically all were victims.

'It reminds me of the Blitz,' said Mr Charley, still with binoculars raised. 'Looking from Primrose Hill over the city.'

I marvelled that he had once been young, in uniform – in a sense, one of Vershinin's 'enemy'. 'What were you doing on Primrose Hill?'

He lowered the binoculars. 'In an ack-ack unit,' he said, and added: 'That fellow wasn't even born then.' The jerk of his head indicated Paul Vickerman's tall silhouette. 'As a matter of fact, I don't suppose you were either.'

'Just about,' I said.

'Can't get used to post-war time. The girls you see around, for instance . . .'

I wondered if Paul divined in the fire some fulfilment of his notion of the Middle East mania being a universal phenomenon. He seemed to be gazing placidly out like the rest of us, but who knows what was going on in his contorted mind? It might well be that Dr Stembridge had come out on the terrace not through common curiosity and *schadenfreude*, but to keep an eye on his more vulnerable patients. Even slightly impinging disasters might be potentially damaging to the regimen at Stares.

There was a male predominance on the terrace, as though we were watching a football match, and I thought, as often in the past, how ameliorated the world might be if controlled by women.

23

I'd been awake since two-thirty, had finished my
book, sleep far away – one of my pill-less nights. It
was a long time since I'd been so caught without the
solace of reading matter, for confidence about sleep
was a new shoot, its strength evidently overestimated.
At length I got up, parted the curtains and looked out
over the lake. Evidence of the fire had gone: instead, a
three-quarters moon hung there, obscured frequently
by moving clouds. I would have gone down to ransack
the books in the library had I not been frightened of
encountering Walter. Yes, I thought, 'frightened' was
the *mot juste*, foolish though it was in the context: I
was frightened of his power to detain and converse, of
his (merely implied) criticism of my being up at such
an ungodly hour – and, indeed, of the life that had
landed me at Stares. Such timidity had inhibited
me in childhood and adolescence and, covertly but
with not much less force, in adult existence. For some,
the actor's temperament was the opposite of this: I
had always envied them, though not knowing how
much could have been mere bravado. But just as I was
trying to convince myself of the folly of fearing a meeting with the egregious night porter, I realized that by
taking the staircase farthest from my bedroom I could
reach the library without passing the desk in the hall. I
put my dressing-gown on, and set quietly forth.

I was due to see Stembridge early the following
morning (actually, it came to me, that morning), and

the anxiety of insomnia was somewhat relieved by the sense that to appear before him pale and pretty shattered would be evidence both of the failure of his regime and my need for support. I thought of Hilary Chiswell going home – to his cat's affection, and the open wound of his bereaved child. For him, the balance had just swung over in favour of a return to life: for myself all still seemed 'Just neutral tinted haps and such'. Contemplating at this dead hour of the twenty-four even the modest enterprise of *The Seagull* reading, I marvelled at the energy that had prompted and sustained me.

Outside the bedroom door I had turned along the corridor the unaccustomed way to reach the farther stairs. The lighting was quite bright, so, when I followed the bend of the corridor, I recognized at once the figure, also dressing-gowned, about to descend the staircase. It was David Waddilove. Quiet as I had been, some noise or sixth sense made him turn his head. I waved my hand from afar, a greeting he sketchily acknowledged. He was probably more embarrassed than I to be caught in this inappropriate nocturnal activity, but had little alternative than to let me catch up with him.

'Are you on the same errand as me?' I asked him.

His hair was tousled over the pale face. 'What?'

'Going down to find something to read. Can't sleep.'

'Oh.' His mind seemed far away, and the effort was visible of his paying attention to the matter in hand. 'I thought I would go for a walk.'

'Does Dr Pentecost allow you sleeping pills? Or perhaps you're against them on principle.'

I had assumed in him the malady of insomnia, but he didn't really address himself to my enquiries.

'I suppose you can get into the grounds during the night.'

'Never tried,' I said. 'Walter would let you out if everywhere was locked up.'

'Walter?'

'The night porter.' There came to me Act II, Scene III of *Macbeth* though there the porter was required to admit not let out. We were descending the staircase so slowly that converse was possible; indeed required. 'I daresay,' I added, 'Walter would get us a hot drink if asked. Though whether he stays awake and available all night remains to be tested.'

'I think I won't go out.'

At the foot of the staircase was a bench with a high back, of dubious antiquity. David sank down on this. For a moment I hesitated, then sat by his side.

'How are things going?'

'All right,' he said. Though there was nothing untoward in their tone, the words seemed to contradict the fact.

'If it's any comfort, my feeling is that the regimen here works for a lot of people, even if pretty slowly. Hilary Chiswell was telling me after dinner he was planning to leave soon. He's the man who was at the Istanbul Airport.'

'Perhaps leaving in despair.'

'Oh no. I'm sure for him the worst is past. Like you, he underwent a terrible trauma.'

'The life here's difficult for me,' he said. 'I'm not used to doing nothing.'

'There are quite a few occupations available.' But it would have seemed ludicrous to have specified snooker, clock-golf, clay-modelling, even the subterranean swimming-bath.

'I work quite hard,' he said. 'Not interested in sport. Though the point of working hard has vanished.'

What could be seen of his pyjama top, beneath his Viyella dressing-gown, was navy-blue, with white piping. I envisaged him at his occupation in equally natty shirting and suiting.

'I'm glad you joined in *The Seagull*. You did very well in the Act IV read-through. No lines for poor Yakov, but a surprising number of stage directions – like some late-Romantic musical score.' Sheer anxiety to reassure him, keep him in going order, lay behind my last remark, its pretentiousness underlined by ignorance as to whether he was any more interested in music than in sport.

He lifted his head and looked at me with candid blue eyes. The lashes were long, the eyebrows almost glistening with the enviable vital essence of youth. 'We always talk about my troubles,' he said. 'Never yours.'

I warmed towards his effort. 'Some day, when you're really on the mend, I'll confide in you.' But I wondered how I could start, delineating a relationship that to many would be incomprehensible if not distasteful.

'Even getting to sleep has its bad side,' he said. 'I dream Elizabeth's alive, then wake and find her dead.'

In Sammy's case I sometimes used to dream I'd lost his love, the sense of loss utterly despairing, contradicting my life. Then when I woke the loss was real.

'But I'm sure that in sleep some healing process goes on,' I said, short of a remark to entice him away from tears. It was strange to be almost whispering with him here, Stares quiet around us, many of its inhabitants still at this hour awake, reading with unseeing eyes as they re-ran the past in their minds; others in the dreamless slumber following their Benquils or whatever, soon to be brought back to reality by a pressure in the bladder or some digestive spasm.

'I wonder if anything can ever heal the sight, the touch, of her blood – so much blood. And I myself unscratched – literally.'

I laid my hand on his arm. 'I have blood in my memory, too.'

Yes, I, too, had been 'stepp'd in blood'. When I'd left David at his bedroom door (we had simply in the end retraced our steps up the staircase and along the corridor) I once again ploughed through the memory of those final days. I was astonished how much I'd already forgotten. What particular drunken virulence from Sammy had sent me from the house that lunchtime and into the car, to drive away at random, trembling, almost weeping with wounded innocence? On his side were the usual irrational accusations of bad behaviour, but with the more recent element apparent of morbid jealousy, quite unfounded.

Eventually, I'd discovered myself on the ring road round Canterbury, decided in an instant to go into the city, half known from years before through a festival engagement. I suppose I would have put my motive down to the attractions of the second-hand bookshops and possibly the antiquities. But wasn't there also even at that stage some notion of possible erotic adventure – not least as revenge for Sammy's accusations or as simple consolation? I found a space in a carpark by the old city walls, wandered into the streets behind the cathedral. In the very first bookshop entered I had some exchange with a young man, merely a matter of politeness over the right of way between shelving and a table of books. Later, sitting in the cathedral purlieus, I saw him arrive and himself sit on another of the benches provided. At the time I marvelled at the coincidence; later, wondered if he hadn't followed me. He knew who I was, but I never found out if it was merely a young man's ardour to know the 'famous' that prompted his eager response when I strolled over and claimed the slight prior acquaintance. We were both carrying recent purchases of books, so that provided the start of a dialogue. A plan had formed even before I'd left my seat – to ask him to dine, to buy a holdall, pyjamas and toothbrush, and book in at an hotel. It was already late afternoon: we arranged to meet in the same place in an hour.

The outcome was not exactly a fiasco, though containing elements of the ridiculous. The boy turned up for the assignation. His name was Julian Treves, reading law but already half a drop-out. It struck me now (as I sat in a reverie on the edge of the bed after saying good-night to David Waddilove, the main bedroom light still on, the bedside lamp still dark) that he was not utterly without resemblance to Paul Vickerman – he might well have preferred 'the Romantic movements of literature' adumbrated in Paul's *curriculum vitae* to what he was actually doing.

We had a few drinks in a pub outside the main gate of the precinct, then found a restaurant. I daresay the boy had had a good deal more to drink than he was used to, but it was well absorbed by food. The whole procedure took me back to strange pre-Sammy days. Instead of ordering it in the restaurant, I asked Julian for coffee to the hotel. He acceded to the invitation. I hadn't made up my mind how to play the remaining moves of the game.

In the lounge I realized at once how staid the hotel was. Well, not quite how staid until a dark-jacketed individual I'd seen behind the desk when I registered came to where we were sitting and asked if he could have a word with me. I imagined some query about my room – a double booking necessitating a move, perhaps. The fellow drew me discreetly to the side of the lounge entrance doors. The first intelligible words I heard from him were: 'We don't usually admit hair of that length, sir.' And I realized that with deference to my status as a hotel resident he was asking me to get rid of my guest as soon as politely convenient, instead of pronto. I looked across the lounge at Julian and immediately saw that in the eyes of the receptionist or sub-manager (and no doubt of the majority of the residents) he was strikingly hairy and scruffy. I did not demur; in fact, felt guilty and ashamed, but that was also due to the evaporation of my plan to take Julian up to my room – as though it had been known to the managerial figure, who was therefore exercising moral authority as well as a somewhat outdated control of mere physical appearance.

Libido thoroughly deflated, I took Julian's telephone number, said I would call him the next morning, though I had to leave fairly early for a rehearsal. So it transpired that I went to my bedroom alone, the night still young. Indeed, from the bedroom window I saw flocks of starlings, two or three of them, high above the city, the spirograph forms showing varying shapes as the wings were presented in full or in profile. It was the screeching of these multitudes that had caused me to open the curtains (which had been drawn by a chamber-maid) and look out. Already some birds were perching on chimney-pots and TV aerials, many momentarily before rejoining the flocks. Then came the actual roosting: ranks of birds in all the available sheltered horizontal spaces – windowsills, decorative mouldings and so on – like an army or political assembly with assigned or traditional places to fill. It occurred to me almost with unease that the sill outside my own window would fill up with the living bodies.

Did my chronic insomnia date from that very night? When I woke in the early hours and failed to drop off again, I got up and looked through the curtains, curious about the starlings. They were clearly visible in the street lights, and like their human counterparts by no means all asleep – some twitching or preening;

two, in fact, engaged in some irascible (possibly marital) mutual pecking. I began to think of Sammy: hitherto, in the entire episode with the boy, he had never once come to mind.

I must have dozed off eventually: when I woke in the early morning the starlings were once more sitting on the aerials and chimneys, presumably gathering to move off in flocks to the city's parks and its suburbs' gardens. I had no more sleep. The motives and desires of the previous day had vanished. I breakfasted as early as I could; thought about ringing Julian, decided to postpone doing it to a more reasonable hour. In any case, it could only be a call of politeness. I retrieved my car and drove back home. I had a script and other oddments to pick up, and I believe I still wanted to try to make things more normal with Sammy. I suppose by that time it was rarely in my mind how attractive he once had been – generous, very funny, the always illuminating comment on anything raised in conversation, especially about the arts, and not only his own. It was as though a bad fairy's gifts had secretly ripened over the years, then suddenly burst out their evil. Some mere *modus vivendi* was perhaps my objective, hoping against hope for better things. In early days with Sammy a friend had said to me – quite by chance, not warning me off – 'one prays Sammy doesn't turn out like his father', and, when questioned, told me that Sammy senior, a music critic whose name I remembered, had declined into an unemployable boozer's late middle-age.

I let myself into the house. All was quiet: no musical sounds. I didn't call: if Sammy was in, let him make the first move. Upstairs, there were disconcerting stains on the landing. On the lighter materials of the bathroom they revealed themselves as blood. I feared to go into Sammy's room, but when I went into my own

—174—

I found him on the floor, his throat cut.

It was that detail – his presence, his dead presence, in my bedroom – that continued to haunt me, along with obvious horrors. Had he planned to give me the worst shock he could envisage, or at the last moment staggered or crawled to get my help, forgetting I'd deserted him? The terrible questions proliferated. The police marvelled that he'd left no note, but Bernard Anderson, who had told me about Sammy's father, said later that the latter also had gone inside the gas cooker without a message.

I could see that the night at Stares, after the dialogue with David, was far different from the night following the encounter with Julian and despite its interruptions and remorse, different from (in a sense more normal than) perhaps any night since I had found Sammy dead. I slept in the end though waking early, and felt I had for once contrived to defeat insomnia quite decisively. My first thought was of amazement that I'd never previously seen the common factor of my night in Canterbury and my coming to Stares – starlings.

24

WHEN I drew the bedroom curtains it was apparent that the Indian summer had broken. Swift clouds were sweeping in from the west; almost as I watched, their colour altering from white to grey. Even indoors it was perceptibly cooler. I was reminded of the alteration in weather in Act IV of *The Seagull*, though it would have been an exaggeration to say, as Masha says, that there were 'huge waves' on the lake.

In the dining-room as I helped myself at the hot-plate, Mr Charley joined me for the same purpose. He was piling some scrambled egg on his plate when he said: 'Do you know what "goosing" is?'

'As a matter of fact, I do.'

'I think the expression came in during the war, when the bloody Yanks arrived. How would you define it?'

Even for Mr Charley this was a distasteful start to a conversation, somehow especially so at breakfast time. But a sharp reaction determined me not to mince matters. 'Shoving a finger *in ano* to shock someone, with sexual intent.'

'Right. Neatly put,' he said. 'Well, Mary Gow's been goosed.'

'Oh, come.'

He accompanied me to a vacant table. 'It's quite true. Mrs Brown told me late last night. Apparently it happened on the terrace while we were watching the fire.'

'Good Lord.'

Mr Charley sneezed three times, each time prolonging the sternutation into an identical musical note. I would have blamed the pepper he had put on his eggs, but as he took his handkerchief away he said: 'I hope I didn't catch cold on that terrace. One disaster is more than enough.'

'Does she know the culprit?'

'Apparently hasn't a clue, what with the darkness and the crowd. Of course, many a girl would have taken it in her stride – so to speak. Thought nothing of it; perhaps been flattered. But our Mary is making a bit of a song and dance.'

'Well, I can see that a young woman doesn't put herself in the charge of Stares to get goosed.'

'You can get goosed anywhere,' said Mr Charley warmly. He had inserted one piece of buttered toast under his eggs, and now generously buttered another. 'You'll be wondering whether this will affect her participation in the play-reading tomorrow.'

'Why should it?'

'It seems she's very upset. Must be suspicious of all the men here, not least the members of the cast.'

I couldn't resist saying: 'What about the women here?'

Mr Charley's attention increased. 'I say, do you think it might have been some covert dyke?'

I felt it was time to calm Mr Charley down. I opened the copy of *The Times* I'd collected as usual from the desk. 'I wonder if there's any report in here about the fire.'

'I listened to the news. It was a fuel dump.'

'Sabotage?'

'Apparently unlikely.' Mr Charley attacked his eggs and toast, but soon put down his knife and fork, and said: 'Naturally, they'll suspect me.'

'Of setting fire to American aviation spirit?'

'No, no.' He took up his knife and fork again. 'Oh, I see. You're pulling my leg.' He added coffee to the eggs and toast in his mouth. 'With my criminal record they're bound to think I was the gooser, though as I think I told you I never got *in ano* or in anything else.'

'Who are "they"? The police?'

'Do you think Mary Gow will make a case of it? Surely not. I mean it was probably no more than a rather over-affectionate caress. No, I was thinking of the authorities here – Stembridge, I suppose, in Mowle's absence.'

'Has she complained?'

'Only to Maida Brown so far as I know. Not a thing she would much want to advertise, I suppose, however flattering to her physical attractions. Funny girl. At first I thought she couldn't say "boo" to a goose so to speak. Accordingly, I was distinctly surprised when she joined in the play, and spoke out loud and clear.'

'I had a similar surprise when she made mincemeat of me at clock-golf,' I said. 'But I hope you're not right about her being put off reading.'

'Who will you get in that event? Miss Stittle, Lady Hargreaves? A trifle elderly for the role, but at least no one will goose them.' Mr Charley cast his eye over the table. 'Can I trouble you for the marmalade?' He regarded the glass dish handed him. 'I wish they'd get some Cooper's Oxford.'

'You don't think Mary imagined the whole thing? That seems much more likely.'

'You mean an extension of her neurosis or whatever it is she's in here for?'

'Yes, rather an extension of hers than someone else's,' I said. 'Perhaps Dr Stembridge will throw some light. My appointment's due after breakfast.'

'Are you having more coffee before you go?'

'No.'

'You wouldn't like to save a poor old man's legs by replenishing my cup? Dark brown, *s'il vous plait*.'

25

'I don't want to try to teach you your job,' I said to Dr Stembridge, as I sat down opposite him at his desk (there was a sofa and adjoining chair in the room, though in my case had never been employed), 'but isn't Paul Vickerman a schizophrenic?'

I'd pondered the least offensive way of opening up the subject, but Stembridge's response was equable. 'We use the term very guardedly these days. Some might class him as having a schizoid personality. But I should say I don't encourage guests to talk of other guests.'

'Of course. But I haven't been happy about Paul in this play-reading taking the part of someone who first tries to kill himself and then succeeds.'

'I don't think you need worry about a bit of play-acting. Bottling-up things does the damage.'

'Then there are these Middle East maniacs. Paul seems to take all that to heart.'

'It often does patients good to find so-called normal people behaving worse than themselves. Besides, it's commonplace for neurotics to bring current matters – politics, as well as books and TV programmes – into their delusional systems.'

I tried to recall other concrete examples of Paul's more than eccentric imaginings and behaviour, but before Dr Stembridge's large, bland presence one's independent powers of thought seemed curiously inhibited. 'Well, don't say I didn't sound a warning note,' I feebly ventured.

'Mr Toyne,' he said, 'don't forget that compared with many here you are a well man. To apply your standards to all and sundry would be unrealistic. Yet they are far from requiring conventional psychiatric detention – or even treatment. We get examples of guests who believe that Military Intelligence or the CIA are bugging their rooms – having craftily transferred the bugging devices from their own homes – and recording any dialogues, or even monologues, so as to be used adversely. Such guests lead otherwise more or less normal lives, and their delusions may be episodic, or actually non-recurring. Who can criticize a wrong suspicion of State surveillance when so much of it goes on in actuality – to say nothing of espionage by quite ordinary citizens? Now let's turn to what we are both here for – the progress of your recovery.'

'I'm not sure what I'm supposed to be recovering from, though it's probably rather late in the day to be saying that.'

'There is one factor you may not have taken enough into account. Do you realize that it's only a year or two ago that the American Psychiatric Association – and not by an overwhelming majority – decided to omit homosexuality from their manual of psychiatric disorders? And that was probably only through the activities of homosexual organizations. Of course, you haven't come here to be weaned from homosexuality, as many patients came to psychiatrists in the past, and so-called homosexual activists are probably distasteful to you. But you are bound, if only subconsciously, to experience guilt still at the depth of your emotion for a homosexual bereavement. That's in addition to the guilt ordinary bereavement brings.'

I felt, not for the first time, that he was not quite on

the ball. Yet the slight obviousness or glibness of what he said made me think afresh about the events that had brought me here, and, above all, of what I should be like when I left. The fat pen adversely commented on by Hilary Chiswell lay beside my folder on the desk, and there were other trappings in the room that might not have stood up well to sceptical scrutiny, yet (perhaps because one's health – destiny, even – was at issue) it was impossible to be other than serious, even faintly awed. Once more, the headmaster and the always potentially erring pupil was the relationship evoked.

I was making a remark that did not quite correspond to what I was thinking when I heard the door open behind me. It was a reflection of my sense of Dr Stembridge's authority that I marvelled that someone could have entered the room in defiance of the red light outside that would undoubtedly be showing. A dire emergency or disaster immediately came to mind as more than likely, so it was with accentuated surprise I recognized the slightly adenoidal voice, not at all unattractive, of Mary Gow.

'I don't know whether you are aware,' she said, 'that I've been indecently assaulted.' The voice trembled, but one guessed more with indignation than nervousness. So long after the actual event, it was plain she had worked herself up to a repetitive peak of emotion.

'I most certainly am not aware,' said Dr Stembridge. His hands been lying relaxedly on the desk before the theatrical entrance: they did not stir. It struck me that he probably thought Mary's words a mere twist to her neurosis, a sexual fantasy.

Mary came into view at the end of the desk. I started half automatically to rise, then copied Stembridge by remaining as I was. 'I expect Bill Toyne knows all about it. The thing's being discussed everywhere, like – like – the blessed Middle East.'

'And do you know about it?' Stembridge asked me, in neutral tones.

'As a matter of fact I do. Someone told me this morning.'

'Who told you?' Mary began to break out, but at this moment Stembridge rose to his imposing height and with slow courtesy ushered her into the second chair that stood by the desk.

'I only got the news second-hand,' I began to Stembridge, but Mary quickly interrupted. Her strength in the situation was as surprising as her prowess at clock-golf.

'You were on the terrace,' she said, addressing Stembridge, like a rude schoolgirl. 'You could have done it. Perhaps you did.'

'Do I take it the identity of the guilty party is so far unknown?' said the doctor.

'This wouldn't have happened if Dr Mowle had been in charge,' cried Mary. 'Everything's worsened since I was here before.'

It was the first time I'd heard that this was not Mary's initial stay at Stares. I saw her troubles reaching far back into childhood. And at the same time the concept came to me, not for the first time, of Duke Mowle mistakenly entrusting morality to Angelo Stembridge. When would the Friar cast off his disguise, expose the guilty and unite the alienated? And even in the, it had to be admitted, sensational (and not altogether lacking in the absurd) confrontation still going on, I remembered the time I played in *Measure for Measure*. It had been a step-up-on-the-ladder part for me – Lucio, the 'Fantastic', the link between the high and low plots. Sammy had come to the first night, afterwards excited by my performance, as I could see. But, as always, there was a certain reticence in his pride and generosity: he would have defended me against criticism, but took his praise as said. Was that the tiny seed of the artistic jealousy that came to echo the physical? When, a good deal later, I showed him an advance copy of my first book, his response was blank.

Dr Stembridge was asking Mary for details of the incident, perhaps an indication of his inward disconcertion that he pursued the matter at such length in my presence. Mary's reply, though far from as blunt as Mr Charley's report had been, was sufficiently explicit to convey to the Deputy Medical Director that the physical side of the affair was not tremendously grave. 'You must remember,' he said to Mary, 'that some at Stares are unbalanced in that very area.' The noun was not well chosen, but quite apt in its way. He went on: 'You're robust enough now mentally to handle these – these incidents – of ordinary life.' I couldn't help thinking that perhaps the remark applied only to Mr Charley's life. 'Here, as I say, we are perhaps more prone to them than elsewhere, you know.'

Mary did not take up the use of 'we' as confirming the possibility of Stembridge's guilt, as I thought she might. For myself, I remembered Angelo's 'Condemn the fault, and not the actor of it? Why, every fault's condemned ere it be done'. Stembridge was departing from the role Mary was casting him in. He certainly came to handle the affair in a highly competent manner – maybe letting me stay so I could note his competence. The nursing sister who assisted with his clinic was summoned, a sedative advised and a promise made that he himself would investigate, and if possible uncover the author of, the offence, admitted to be heinous, despite any proneness to goosing fellow patients to be expected in those at Stares. When Mary had left in the nurse's care, I said: 'I don't know whether you're aware of it or not, but Dr Mowle's absence is having quite an effect. You heard Mary Gow's remark just now. I've heard other speculations. And even if he returned I think Paul Vickerman would imagine him to be not the real Medical Director but an impostor.'

Dr Stembridge smiled with what I took to be considerable self-control. 'That syndrome is well-known, of course. It may be familiar to you through the life of the poet Cowper. During one episode of break-down he was convinced that his friend Parson Newton had been replaced by a substitute. In fact, for the rest of his life he could never be sure if the Newton he saw was the real Newton or some phantom masquerading in Newton's bodily shape. But I doubt if Vickerman is far down that road.'

Once again the reason for Dr Mowle's absence was being withheld. The conversation with Fred Boraston came back to me, when we had speculated rather fancifully about the Resident Medical Director's non-appearance. The goosing of Mary Gow had failed to dent Dr Stembridge's phlegm: why shouldn't I press him on the mystery of Dr Mowle?

'Nevertheless, I've spoken to several people, less *outré* than Paul, who are concerned that they can't see the physician they expected to see – with all due respect to you and the rest of the medical staff.'

'Geoffrey Mowle is under extreme pressure at the moment in his private life. He'll be back here just as soon as it's humanly possible. He knows only too well the difficulties his absence makes, both for the staff and for his patients.'

'I must say I would have thought it best to come clean about his being away. All sorts of fantasies are in course of fabrication.'

'I would give anyone who asked me the direct question a straight answer,' said the doctor.

'Well, I ask it.'

'Dr Mowle is an only son. Both his parents have terminal cancer, now in their last days. I'm sure you appreciate his obligations and concern, for it is your nature also to be scrupulously conscientious.'

I may well have gone red, both at the analysis of my character and my probing into Dr Mowle proving so painful. 'I'm truly sorry.'

'It's wiser not to spread the news, don't you think?'

Was the Resident Medical Director not to be revealed as having bereavements and family traumas like the rest of us, even if on a grander scale? 'You know best.'

'Well,' said Dr Stembridge, 'your session this morning has been subject to a few vicissitudes, and now your time's nearly up.'

'Hilary Chiswell tells me he's going home.'

'Yes, that's his decision.'

'I suppose I shall have to make my decision in the not too distant future.'

'How's the sleeping?'

I considered. 'Tolerable.'

'You don't want with your own doctor to get back into a routine of Benquil – or anything else, for that matter. I will philosophize generally. As you move deeper into middle-age you must learn to give thanks for every day you wake alive, whatever may lie in store. Then you will have formed good habits for old age. And never forget life really isn't in places like Stares. It is where you can enjoy – and by that I mean cope with – all the things we forbid you or discourage you from here.'

'Like goosing girls?'

Stembridge laughed. 'Like whisky and flirtations

and over-work and rich food.'

'So that's what life is.'

'Think things over for a few days – I mean about returning to it.'

There was a blatter of rain on the big windows. I imagined waves possibly on the lake. 'Our famous play-reading takes place tomorrow evening. I shall see that through at least.'

'I hope to attend.'

'We shall be nervous and honoured.'

When I left, I found Maida Brown waiting her turn outside. I said to her: 'The doctor knows about the *contretemps* on the terrace last night.'

'I should bloody well hope so. If a girl can't enjoy watching a fire without being poked up the arse it's a poor do.'

'I don't know how you expect Stares to be able to guard against that sort of thing.'

'Well, they needn't accept clients like John Charley.'

'I doubt if Mr Charley was the culprit.' At that instant it struck me that Noel Mummery might have succumbed to a wicked impulse. 'Mary herself thinks it might have been the doctor.' I couldn't resist the exaggeration.

'Singh? Sounds too much like the plot of *A Passage to India*.'

'Not Singh, Stembridge.'

'What, has she actually confronted her assailant?'

Luckily the green light went on before I was drawn into further indiscretion, and Maida went in to her appointment. What she might say to Stembridge made an interesting speculation.

As usual, an institution – outwardly so impersonal – eventually reveals itself full of human traits; flaws and inefficiencies in particular making themselves incongruously manifest. That Dr Mowle was simply ushering his agonized mother and father out of the world was on the whole more surprising than if he had been fraudulent or mad. The staff at Stares, with whatever awe one had at first regarded them, were cut from the same cloth as the rest of us – from Denise's (presumed) adultery, through Noel's abstract paintings (surely a quasi-insane aberration of art) to Dr Pentecost's flashy motor-car and Dr Singh's tropical suitings. It might be argued that they were all candidates for exchanging roles with those in their care.

'You are conscientious,' pronounced Stembridge. It was a diagnosis I would not have made myself. How unlikely that I should have been assiduous at the deathbeds of my parents! Yet why didn't I leave Sammy once it was plain he had lost his love for me, even acquired hate – to say nothing of his impossible conduct day by day? The mechanics of separation were no bar: he could have gone on living where he was, and I was earning enough to set myself up in a new establishment.

'You are a romantic,' Stembridge might well have said. Sometimes, when half way through the evening Sammy had bad-temperedly gone off to bed to fall into drunken sleep, I would get the car out and drive to a place where I had happened previously to have seen an attractive boy. It was an action without outcome, such as I'd taken in adolescence. Looking back, it seemed the action of a dotty simpleton. No wonder I was at Stares.

And as to money, I now seemed awash with it. A paradox of bereavement was that it often materially enriched the bereaved. When Dr Mowle had ushered his mother and father across the Styx he might feel some compensation in inheriting their estates. I couldn't pretend to have been indifferent to the surprising value of Sammy's estate – and the extent of the royalties that I was starting to see arrive, most notably from his brilliant, nearly too Elgarian orchestration of the Elgar organ sonata that had almost come to be regarded as a third symphony. That aspect of his life he had never revealed to me – and apart from legacies to nephews and nieces, I was his sole beneficiary. Did he never really cease to love me, or was altering his will just one of the several chores that in his disorganized latter days he never got round to carrying out?

By a singular coincidence, Dr Singh, on what seemed to have become his regular pre-lunch appearance, touched on the matter later that morning. I was in the hall with Fred Boraston when the doctor, passing through, stopped where we were sitting. He was so short he had no need to sit down himself to converse at ease with us.

'Don't drink too much carrot juice,' he said, eyeing our drinks. 'You can quite soon imbibe an excess of Vitamin A, as well as turning yellow.'

'Good grief, don't tell me carrot juice is as dangerous as the aperitifs it replaces in this establishment,' I said.

'One deleterious thing it won't effect,' said the doctor, his smile revealing some gold dentistry, less sophisticated than Mr Boraston's, 'is loss of memory. I have just been reading an interesting paper on the way excessive alcohol consumption affects the nerve cells of the brain. The suggestion is that the alcohol does not damage all nerve cells equally, but rather those associated with memory loss – the class that signal to one another, if you'll forgive the technical expression, through the action of the acetylcholine neurotransmitter.'

'How on earth has that been brought to light?'

'Rats,' said Dr Singh, complacently. 'The rat is a good model for humans. It rapidly becomes addicted to alcohol, even under stress chooses alcohol in prefer-ence to water. When the rat has developed what we call in humans Korsakoff's syndrome, it finds it hard to discover its way through a simple maze – even after a month on the wagon.'

'You're alarming us.' I remembered Mr Chiswell making a similar observation in less scientific terms.

'But there's a cure. For rats, at any rate. A brain transplant of nerve cells of the type containing acetylcholine.'

'Thank goodness.'

'You're laughing at me,' said Dr Singh, good humouredly. 'However, if accurate brain tissue trans-plants in humans became practicable they might, for example, reverse the effects of Alzheimer's disease or Parkinsonism.'

Rather as in the case of the labial herpes, I was almost expecting him to diagnose those conditions in me. However, with a little tap on my shoulder, he moved on.

'You're not under him, are you?' I asked Fred Boraston.

'No. But I can see he might do some people a lot of good. It seems he was formerly in practice in East Africa. He said that the neuroses there were like those in Freud's Vienna. Can you believe it?'

'Idle women with servants, and so forth.'

'I suppose so. Even a black bourgeoisie with servants, or what have you.' We both laughed: 'and so forth' and 'or what have you' were my versions of Sorin's catch-phrases. I noticed Mr Boraston was carrying a book. 'I see you finished *Mansfield Park*, perhaps abandoned it,' I remarked. 'I was thinking only this morning of that first conversation we had by the lake.'

'Oh, I ploughed through it to the bitter end. Not

very likely now that Dr Mowle's unexpected appearance will put paid to the performance of our play. It seems quite a long time ago, that conversation.'

'We move on here, almost without knowing it.' I seemed to have said this before to someone.

'Yes, and I suppose feeling easier with people is a measure of our progress. We look back at the odd and even foolish things we may have come out with – never to be repeated – but surely having had their effect.'

Doubtless his confidences about Maida came into such a category. It struck me forcibly at this moment that many of us arrived at Stares having experienced, still expecting, strange conjunctions in their lives – a kind of existence it was the business of Stares to try to reduce to ordinary dimensions. Dr Mowle was not fraudulent or mad; Maida was not Fred's long-lost daughter. Yet of course the bizarre could not be completely removed from life: Mary got goosed; the Arts Director met the *maîtresse d'hôtel* in the boathouse.

Someone came in through the front-door and admitted also a few windblown leaves. 'Autumn has arrived in a day,' remarked Mr Boraston.

I thought how he had revealed in the last few days almost a poetic side to his character. Then he made some remarks that further surprised me. 'Isn't it strange? With neither of my wives did I ever get round to discussing the truly serious things of life – I mean the secret parts of one's existence.'

'Are they the truly serious things?'

'Oh yes.'

'I wonder. Sometimes I feel nothing is truly serious except the awful.'

26

I imagined, as one often does about the future, each step of 'going home' – from packing up here to finding my now quite unfamiliar key and opening the door. I thought about getting back into condition, as they say – the state, so comparatively easy to achieve in the past, of readiness for any physical demand of the profession, even merely seven performances a week. I envisaged regularly riding again, fencing again – postponing the decline into middle-aged character parts. I could renew singing lessons, for these days a musical might be made out of anything, even Chekhov. Were such things within my grasp? In a way they seemed even more remote than turning out a professional piece of writing, that really not long ago had become an absorbing part of life – writing that was moving from dialogue to reflection, a revelation of what had accumulated almost unknowingly in my mind since childhood. Once more one had to ask oneself if this very absorption hadn't led, through alienating Sammy, to its present opposite. And as to fitness, the irony came back of actually once, at the injustice of his accusations, biffing him, and finding astonishingly that I was then by far the stronger, so much so that I soon desisted.

This reverie occurred as I lay on my bed in the late afternoon. Following lunch, I'd prepared a programme for the play-reading – simply a sheet with the cast list, and a brief note about Chekhov and the play, that

Noel had arranged for the office to photocopy. One says 'office', but the business involved my penetrating to the floor where in earlier times Dr Mowle or the ants-seeing man were half seriously said to be incarcerated. There were doors marked 'Enquiries' and 'Administrator'. I handed in my piece of paper to a small world of staff and machines which closer acquaintance would no doubt have revealed as being as human and fallible – even as dotty – as the play's *dramatis personae*. The office was to pass the copies on to Noel, who would distribute them to the audience, presumably by laying them on the seating.

Then I'd come to my room, stretched on the bed, read a little, and next, instead of as usual these days, immediately feeling wide awake again, with throbbing head, drifted off into sleep – so prolonged, in fact, that I'd missed the tea hour. The ability to sleep at that time took me back to former days, snoozing between matinée and evening performance, waking with an energy felt right down to the toes. I was to see *The Seagull* readers briefly after dinner, before the evening entertainment, when they would be available for morale-boosting and last-minute queries. Noel Mummery had now procured individual copies of Chekhov for each member of the cast; his further visit to the town might well have coincided with Denise's time off, catering duties making assignations difficult. Before dinner I was staring out at the rain gluing the fallen leaves to the paving of the terrace when I was aware of Lady Hargreaves at my side, her bent figure far short of even my too modest height.

'Come and have a drink,' she said, 'if such a name can be given to the stuff served here.'

Mindful of Dr Singh's warning, I chose aerated apple juice and took it with her tomato juice to seats in the hall, accommodating my pace to her aged hobble.

'I'm looking forward to your play tomorrow, not least wondering how everyone will come out. When my husband was alive we went regularly to the great repertory theatres, he being so prominent in the arts world. I was always fascinated by seeing the same actors in a succession of different roles.'

'I'm afraid here you'll only see real life and one other.'

'What a pity you can't follow up *The Seagull* with Ibsen, for example. Oh, I shouldn't say "what a pity" – that would be condemning you longer to Stares, whereas I'm sure you're preparing to go back home and your proper acting life.'

'One lives in hope.'

'Hope. Yes, that's the thing. So little of it at my age, in my condition.' She had evidently been out in the rather wild weather, and, though discarding her coat somewhere indoors, had kept her hat on, a fairly small affair, which had allowed her grey locks to become windblown. She was conscious of its inadequacies, for every now and then she resettled it on her head, though without effecting any real improvement. This increasing dishevelment was the only detectably unbalanced thing about her, but, after all, sane appearance counts for much in the world. 'When your husband dies no one wants you. Especially in my case. When we first married, Malcolm had quite a modest place in society. Me, too. He made a name under his own steam. Do you see what I mean?' Some Midlands accent lurked under her speech, probably revealing itself the more with her rising feeling.

'Absolutely.'

She sipped her tomato juice. It left a line on her upper lip even more ill-drawn than her lipstick. 'I read in some book,' she said, 'forgotten where, about someone whose gestures and caresses entailed an enormous effort on her part, because she was so shy, and yet were taken for granted by the recipient, probably not thought nearly effort enough. That was the story of my life. And isn't it funny that in old age, when no one wants my love, I feel I could express it quite easily?'

'I wonder if you are right to think people don't want you.'

She took the point. 'Well, I may be just passable in my self – at least, I was not long ago – but there is all the difficult business of finding a spare man for dinner or a spare fourth at bridge. And who wants to call on you to hear the same old woes, the story of the same old daily round?'

'Actually, I'm also now alone in the world.'

'Ah, but it's different for a man. And you have your work. Isn't it strange? – I never had a proper job. I was married straight from home. After school I just helped in my father's shop, or with the housework and my younger siblings. Could hardly happen today, could it?'

'I should think you were good university material.'

'Since I've lived alone I've got very talkative when the opportunity occurs. Not that I'm the only one here to talk a lot. Has Lorna Cochrane told you about her affairs? Yes, well it now seems that she's going to buy a house for her sister's son – Mrs Doggett's son, that awful woman who came here – and he'll take Mrs Doggett off Lorna's hands. That's the theory. Let's trust the bribe will work. It reminds me of that Kipling poem, you know. How does it go?'

' "Once you have paid him the Dane-geld You never get rid of the Dane".'

'That's exactly it. How clever of you to know it!'

'I once read it in a radio programme.'

'We all seem to know one another's affairs here. I

suppose it's partly through being encouraged by the doctors to tell our troubles. And then some are lonely, no one to talk to in the normal course of things.' She laid her hand, with its historical rings, on my arm. 'I often think: we've all been singled out by Fate.'

'The Ship of Fools.'

'Yes,' she said eagerly, 'but what was that, exactly?'

'It was to take the voyagers to the Land of Fools.'

She tried to push back a fallen wisp of hair under her hat. 'It doesn't quite fit in, does it? And yet . . .'

I was not sorry to hear the gong sound for dinner, and rather hoped Denise would separate us when we presented ourselves at the dining-room.

27

THE central heating remained remorseless through the night. However wide the bedroom window had been opened, and even after visiting the subterranean bath, one felt by the time one had dressed and gone downstairs a longing for fresh air before breakfast. The next morning I went out on the puddled terrace, and then, the rain having apparently ceased, down the steps to the garden. The gardener was coming down one of the paths. When he reached me, he said: 'What a terrible thing about that young man!'

My stomach gave a lurch. 'I haven't heard . . .'

'It was me 'at found him. Terrible shock it was, I can tell you.'

No doubt I'd always half stifled the uneasy sense that, prompted by his role in the play, Paul might kill himself. Had I absolutely clearly been absolved from guilt by Stembridge's go-ahead? In that awful moment, too, I had no doubt that the gardener had 'found' him drowned in the lake. But the jockey-like figure went rapidly on, intent on rehearsing and perfecting his sensational tale: 'I'm here before seven. That's always been my way of working. When I passed the row of garages I heard an engine, sounded like the choke was out. But all the garage doors was shut. I opens the one in question – not locked – and the place is full of fumes. When they've cleared, I go in to switch the engine off and sees a piece of hose stuck in a rear window-light from the exhaust. Then I knew something was up, and sure enough this young chap was lying on the back seat. It wasn't a bit of any of my hoses, I may say. He must have brought it with him when he came.'

Perhaps in deference to his discovery he was carrying his greasy cap in his hands. The deep brown tints of his face finished half way up his brow; the rest of that insignificant feature, and the sparsely grey-stranded skull, being pallid. 'Was he dead?' The question seemed expected, if otiose. I thought: he should never have been entrusted with a lethal weapon like a car.

'Aye. Of course, I saw one of the doctors was called straight away. What a shock to see him laying there, his face an' all. Mind you, I'm not surprised at something like that happening here. I'm just going for a bit of breakfast, then I've got to see the coroner's officer when he comes . . .'

But what his other movements were to be I didn't stay to hear. With a word of excuse I went back towards the house, eager for details of the repercussion, and for reassurance, absolution. It was an indication of my anxiety that, encountering him on the terrace, I was prepared to question Mr Charley. 'Have you heard about Paul Vickerman?'

'No. What about him?' His not altogether logical reply was somewhat abstracted, as though, contrary to character, he did not welcome the opportunity of conversation.

'Found dead in his car.'

'No, no. You've been given duff gen. It was that young fellow David Whatshisname – Waddilove.'

'You mean Paul is all right?'

'As far as I know,' said Mr Charley. 'It's certainly the other young fellow who's dead. The news came straight from the administration office.' Though presumably he had only stepped outdoors for a breath of air, he was wearing the deer-stalker hat he affected. 'There's a fair amount of controlled panic indoors. Not going to do the reputation of the place any good.'

The question still arose: had the play-reading prompted the death? 'I talked to David the night before last. He appeared not too bad.' The words seemed feebly self-exculpatory, though probably any words would. I tried to remember some of the things he said, but most vivid was the image of his slender neck emerging from the smart pyjamas and dressing-gown. The mention of the rear window-light indicated that though he had all too appropriately killed himself with a motor-car, it could not have been the MG that had probably been a write-off anyway.

'First, the goosing of Mary Gow, and now this,' said Mr Charley. 'What next? Such things often go in threes.'

'You forget the conflagration. This is the third.'

'So it is.' Mr Charley turned to follow me indoors. He said: 'I remember when things seemed important, now no more.'

'Not even death?'

'Only my own.'

I wasn't yet at that stage of life, I thought. When I found Sammy dead the unique and grotesque at once became the normal: one rose to the challenge, the crisis, the horror presented, finding from somewhere, previously unplumbed, a special energy and resource that enabled one not only to continue with existence but also to match its sudden and unprecedented demands. David's death called for little of this from me: it was his parents who would have to rearrange their lives. He himself had just failed to make such a rearrangement.

28

'I got your note about the play-reading,' said Fred Boraston. I had put in their pigeonholes behind the desk in the hall a word of cancellation to all those I hadn't been able to speak to. There was a similar notice for the potential audience on the notice-board by the dining-room entrance. 'Naturally, I didn't expect it to take place in the circumstances.' Boraston was standing in the hall, wearing a nice Burberry.

'I thought I would set everyone's mind at rest.'

'Are you off out or just coming in? Stembridge has cancelled his appointments for this morning, so I'm at a loose end for half an hour. But perhaps you'd prefer to walk alone.'

'No, I'd like to come with you. I want to avoid brooding on that death, if possible.'

'If I may say so, I'm sure no one attaches any blame to the play.'

'No better choice than *Lovers' Vows*, as it turned out.'

'Certainly as ill-fated.'

When we moved off the terrace the wind caught my hair, grown rather long at Stares. Mr Boraston had provided himself with a soft hat that matched his Burberry. Despite his being a fellow patient, he seemed much better equipped for life than I. 'This takes me back to that morning when we first really talked together.'

'Yes,' I said. 'I was rather in awe of you.'

'Really?' He was amused. 'Years ago I heard that one of our assistant solicitors had made precisely that remark. It came as a not altogether pleasant surprise. Thereafter I tried, when I thought about it, to be more lenient. But young solicitors, to say nothing of articled clerks, do tend to make awful cock-ups.'

'Thanks goodness I'm not an assistant solicitor.'

'Of course,' said Mr Boraston, 'the boot was on the other foot when you were conducting the play-readings. Shall we ever give the performance, do you think?'

'Well, our poor Yakov has gone, and Hilary Chiswell is soon departing, he says. So . . .'

We passed into the park, where the fallen leaves shone with the recent rain. Mr Boraston said: 'Things seem fated not to – to conjoin.'

I wondered if he was thinking of his long-lost daughter. 'No, we shall never know how *The Seagull* would have flown – or died. And probably, who goosed Mary Gow.'

'Oh, you heard about that, did you?' he said.

'Little seems to remain secret at Stares.' Except, I thought, those revelations that would for ever stay in the physicians' files.

'I suppose if it wasn't mere self-deception,' said Mr Boraston, 'Mr Charley must be the prime suspect.'

'It is rather an Agatha Christie situation.'

'Talking of the devil . . .' Coming from the lake, on a path that would converge with ours, was Mr Charley. There may have been some significance in our not taking avoiding action as on the previous occasion Fred Boraston and I had walked together.

'You know,' I said, 'though it sounds pretentious, even ludicrous, I wonder if he isn't happier among the dead.'

'You mean young Waddilove?'

'Yes.'

'It may be so, but one wouldn't quite choose it for oneself,' said Mr Boraston.

'I suppose that's why we're here, to try to avoid that choice.' As he approached us, Mr Charley raised his arm in possibly mock-Nazi salute, and then fell in with our march.

'I hope you're not going too far,' he said. 'I've already been half way round the lake.'

'I expect you've been checking the management of the estate,' I said facetiously, referring to his part in *The Seagull*.

'Well,' he said, with surprising resource, 'there will be no horses to spare to relieve your weary legs.'

We walked on in silence for a while, then Mr Charley's falsetto quietly arose:

Because God made thee mine I'll cherish thee-hee,
Through light and darkness, through all time to
   be . . .

I glanced over to Fred Boraston: a flicker of complicity appeared on his countenance. But then, were the minor or comic characters any more absurd than the protagonists?

And pray a wider world of hope and joy I see
Because you come to me.

I nearly said, when Mr Charley's singing ceased for the time being: all's an illusion, all's a play, sentiments once voiced by Mr Chiswell; but I thought better of it.